O9-AHW-978

ELLE KENNEDY

Millionaire's Last Stand

ROMANTIC

SUSPENSE

Recycling programs
for this product may
not exist in your area.

ISBN-13: 978-0-373-27756-8

MILLIONAIRE'S LAST STAND

www.Harlequin.com

Printed in U.S.A.

Books by Elle Kennedy

ELLE KENNEDY

A RITA® Award-nominated author, Elle Kennedy grew up in the suburbs of Toronto, Ontario, and holds a B.A. in English from York University. From an early age, she knew she wanted to be a writer, and actively began pursuing that dream when she was a teenager. She loves strong heroines and sexy alpha heroes, and just enough heat and danger to keep things interesting.

Elle loves to hear from her readers. Visit her website, www.ellekennedy.com, for the latest news or to send her a note.

To Patience and Keyren,
for giving my millionaire hero a chance!

Prologue

We've got a body.

The call had come in on his cell phone, jolting him from restless slumber, and as he'd left his barren farmhouse and driven over, he hadn't been able to fight the dread climbing up his chest. Now it was jammed in the back of his throat and refused to dislodge. An omen that his peaceful little town was about to become...well, not so peaceful anymore.

Patrick "Finn" Finnegan killed the engine of his Jeep and stared out the windshield at the commanding mansion up ahead. Situated on the edge of a rocky cliff, the house resembled a smaller version of a medieval castle. Rumor had it Cole Donovan had wanted to use wood to make the structure akin to the rustic homes that were trademark to the area, but his wife had demanded the house be made of stone.

Finn wasn't surprised. Teresa Donovan always acted like a queen, so why not live as one?

A rap on the driver's window jarred him from his thoughts.

Finn looked up to see Anna Holt, his most dedicated deputy. Uneasiness swam in Anna's astute brown eyes, the stiffness of her slim body hinting at what Finn expected to find inside the extravagant home.

"How bad is it?" he said in lieu of a greeting as he slid out of the driver's seat.

Anna hesitated. "Bad," she finally said.

The two of them walked up the limestone path leading to the pillared entrance of the mansion. They moved through the ornate double doors, which were filigreed with bronze and more suited to the entry of a cathedral than a home in North Carolina. Inside the spacious front hallway, a white marble floor stretched beneath Finn's black boots, another incongruity considering the home's granite exterior. Teresa Donovan had evidently opted for a show of wealth rather than consistency.

"She's in here," Anna said, gesturing to the arched doorway on their left.

As they crossed the threshold, Finn rubbed the stubble on his chin and cast a weary look across the lavishly furnished living room where his second deputy, Max Patton, stood by the enormous black slate fireplace, dusting the mantle and the framed photographs atop it for fingerprints. Finn's gaze zeroed in on one particular photo, which showed a beaming Teresa in a wedding gown, flanked by a tall man with olive-colored skin and dark eyes.

Cole Donovan, real estate tycoon, ex-husband and possible murder suspect.

Finn suppressed a groan. Damn it. This was the last thing his town needed. In the five years he'd served as the sheriff of Serenade, there hadn't been a single murder. People simply didn't get killed here.

With a sigh, Finn finally forced himself to focus on the main event, the lifeless body of Teresa Donovan.

Even in death she was a beautiful woman, with her black hair fanned out on the parquet floor like strands of fine silk. The wide-set eyes beneath her closed lids had once been stormy silver but he knew they were now a lifeless gray, and her skin, once milky-white, had a bluish tinge to it. She wore a wine-colored peignoir, short enough to reveal her firm lower thighs and shapely calves. She wasn't a tall woman, but her flawless beauty had always made her seem larger than life.

So had her volatile personality.

"Got something under the fingernails" came the medical examiner's nasal voice.

Finn frowned. "She scratched the guy?"

Len Kirsch shrugged, his wire-rimmed glasses sliding down the bridge of his long, thin nose. "Possibly. But you could wind up with skin cells under the fingernails from just caressing someone's arm. I'll examine the body more thoroughly at the lab to check for concrete defensive wounds."

Another sigh lodged in Finn's chest. Christ. Why did it have to be *this* woman? It would be hard finding even one person in town who'd liked Teresa. Hated her? Well, the numbers in that camp would make most of the town a suspect.

He stared at the neat little hole in Teresa's nightie. Right in the heart. Someone hadn't been screwing around here. The shot had been meant to kill.

He rose to his feet, while the lone forensics tech employed by the Serenade Police Department snapped photos of the scene. The rest of the living room was pristine. No overturned furniture, no hints of a struggle. The only sign of foul play was the body lying on the floor next to the brown leather couch, and the ominous pool of blood congealing on the hardwood.

Damn Cole Donovan. He'd caused nothing but trouble since moving to Finn's town two years ago. Shut down the paper mill and built a hotel in its place. Married Serenade's ultimate bad girl. Divorced her.

And quite conceivably killed her.

This was a quiet town. Serenade's five thousand or so citizens were pleasant, hardworking people. They quietly lived their lives, they raised their families and attended the annual craft festival every August, they ran the quaint shops on Main Street and catered to the tourists that wandered into their picturesque town.

Cole Donovan wasn't one of them. He was a big-city man. He'd built his real estate empire in Chicago, then taken it up and down the Atlantic Seaboard, developing in little towns that didn't appreciate his interference.

With growing weariness Finn's gaze was yet again drawn to Teresa's body, and as he stared at the pool of sticky, crimson blood gathering next to it, only one thought entered his mind.

All hell is about to break loose.

Chapter 1

Two Weeks Later

"Are you sure you don't want me to stay?" Ian Macintosh asked, hesitating in the doorway of Cole Donovan's isolated house.

"Go back to Chicago," Cole answered with a sigh. He held up his hand before his assistant could object. "I'll be fine, Ian. Worst thing the sheriff will do is arrest me."

Ian's face went cloudy. "I don't know how you're so calm about this, boss. If I were being wrongfully accused of something, I'd lash out at the entire damned department." He flushed. "Don't tell my mum I said that. She's spent twenty-five years trying to instill good manners in me."

Uh-oh, Ian must really be worried about him, if his British accent was flaring up. Cole had hired the kid on a business trip to London, during which Ian had pulled him aside at a conference and told him he wanted nothing more than to be a part of Donovan Enterprises. Cole had his reservations at first—the kid was barely out of college—but over the past five years, Ian had proven to be invaluable.

Which was why Cole needed him back in Chicago, overseeing everything at the company's headquarters while Cole tried to put an end to this mess he'd found himself in.

Damn Teresa. Although a part of him was still reeling over the fact that his ex-wife was dead, there was also a small part that thought *good riddance.* That woman had caused him nothing but trouble over the past two years. She'd hurt him, humiliated him, cost him not only money, but pride.

And now she was gone, and Sheriff Finnegan lurked in the shadows with a pair of handcuffs, just waiting for the moment he could arrest Cole.

He stifled a groan, resisting the urge to pull out his own hair. He needed to squash this situation before it got completely out of hand. The papers had already gotten a whiff of the story, and the last thing he needed right now was negative publicity. Donovan Enterprises had taken a hit in the market thanks to the recession, and he couldn't afford to have prospective developments fall through because Serenade's sheriff had decided he was a killer.

"Make sure you contact Kurt Hanson when you get in," Cole said as he followed Ian out onto the wraparound porch of the house. "Take him to dinner, pump him with wine and confidence. We can't have him backing out of the waterfront deal."

Ian busily keyed the instructions into his BlackBerry, efficient as always. He glanced up, his brown eyes grave. "And what about the Warner hotel? Kendra Warner decided to double the price on the property. Are we going to meet the new figure?"

Cole rubbed his chin, mulling over the question as the two men walked toward Ian's rental car. "No," he finally said.

"The property isn't worth it. Add a million to the bid, and if she puts up a fight, tell Margo to look for another location."

Ian's fingers flew over the BlackBerry's keyboard. "Okay. I'll call you when I get in." The younger man opened the driver's door of the rented sedan, sending a concerned glance over his shoulder. "I could stay," he said again.

"Go," Cole said firmly. "I can handle this mess by myself."

With a resigned smile, Ian slid into the driver's seat and started the engine. Cole drifted back to the porch, waved stiffly as Ian drove off, then headed back inside. The moment the door closed behind him, his shoulders sagged, heavy with the stress and shock of the past two weeks.

Teresa was dead.

The woman he'd been married to for two years was *dead*.

So why didn't he feel anything but relief?

He keyed in the code on the panel by the door to set the security alarm, then walked into the living room and made his way to the wet bar in the corner of the room. His hands were annoyingly shaky as he grabbed a glass and dumped a few ice cubes into it, followed by a hefty amount of bourbon. He glanced at the intricate wooden grandfather clock across the spacious room. Four o'clock. Wonderful. He'd resorted to drinking in the middle of the afternoon. To *drinking,* period. He never indulged in alcohol, not since his college graduation, which he'd left early in order to drive his mother to rehab.

Cole's legs grew as heavy as his shoulders. He moved toward one of the two black leather couches and sank down, lifting his glass to his lips. The alcohol stung his throat as it slid down to his gut, where it burned his insides.

He drank in silence, wishing, and not for the first time, that he'd never laid eyes on Teresa Matthews. One night, that's all it had taken for him to fall for the woman. Six months later they were married.

A year after that, filing for divorce.

He was just draining his drink when the sound of a car engine drifted in from the open window. Ian was the only other person who had the codes for the steel gate at the end of the driveway, which meant his assistant was coming back. Probably left something behind.

Sighing, Cole set his glass on the coffee table and stood up, frowning when a flash of black crossed his peripheral vision. He turned to the window, and his eyes narrowed as he spotted an unfamiliar SUV emerging from the long dirt driveway on the property.

Damn Ian. This was the second time his assistant had forgotten to arm the gate on his way out. What was the point in paying for an overly expensive security system when his own staff couldn't lock a damn gate?

The SUV's windows were tinted, so he couldn't see the driver, but whoever it was drove up and parked right beside his pickup. The engine shut off, and then the driver's-side door opened and an exceptionally attractive redhead stepped out. She wore a fitted black business suit that showed off her tall, willowy form, complete with slacks that hugged her long legs and a jacket left unbuttoned to reveal the crisp white-collared shirt beneath it. Very professional, save for the auburn-colored hair casually cascading over her shoulders and resting well below her breasts.

Cole's breath hitched slightly when the woman started to walk. She had a long, confident gait. She moved with her shoulders straight, her chin high, as if she had no care in the world and should she *have* a care, she'd just kick its ass.

She disappeared from view as she approached the porch, and Cole immediately banished the brief spark of lust from his groin. He marched to the front hall, ducking into a small room to the right where he swiftly punched in the code to close and lock the front gate, then glanced at the dozen security monitors that displayed various parts of the property. There was nothing out of the ordinary on the screens, save for the gorgeous redhead standing on his porch.

When the doorbell rang, he was back to his current state of wary and pissed off. Chances were, this woman was just another reporter, following in the footsteps of her predecessors and trying to get a juicy interview.

Well, screw that. He was tired of strangers demanding answers, prying into his business.

Back stiff, he yanked open the front door and fixed a deadly scowl at the redhead. "No comment," he snapped.

She blinked in surprise. Then she smiled. "Did I ask for a comment?"

Cole was momentarily taken aback. That smile…damn, it lit up her whole face. Not only that, but it contained only warmth and sincerity, and none of the smug self-interest most reporters tended to exude.

"Oh, you think I'm a reporter," she said knowingly. The smile widened, and then her full red lips parted to release a melodic laugh. "Sorry to disappoint. And I apologize for not pressing that little intercom button at the gate. It was open, so I figured it was okay to drive in."

He opened his mouth to speak, but nothing came out. He was too mesmerized by her eyes, which he now noticed were a dark shade of violet. She was beautiful, but in an unconventional way. Her eyes were tilted up at the corners, making her seem exotic, but her straight, aristocratic nose and perfectly shaped mouth brought elegance to her features. The sprinkling of freckles on her cheeks made her seem wholesome. Exotic, elegant and wholesome. Definitely a peculiar trio. Add to that the long, smoking hot body and this woman, whoever she was, made for a stunning and interesting package.

"Who are you?" he asked, finally finding his voice.

She flashed another smile. "Jamie Crawford." Reaching into her jacket pocket, she pulled out a small leather ID case and flipped it open. "FBI."

Well, he didn't *look* like a killer, Jamie thought ruefully as she forced herself not to drool over the incredible man standing in front of her. Man? Movie star was more like it. He had olive-toned skin, dark, almost black, eyes, and chocolate-brown hair that curled slightly under his ears. And the blue T-shirt and faded jeans that hung low on his trim hips revealed a lean, muscular body that didn't seem to suit a powerful real estate mogul.

She'd expected Donald Trump and got Johnny Depp instead.

Along with a spark of unwanted awareness, which she quickly tamped down.

This wasn't a blind date, for Pete's sake. She was here to interview a suspect. A *murder* suspect, to boot.

The reminder only strengthened when the eyes of the man in front of her darkened to an angry charcoal. "FBI," he echoed. "Wonderful. So the sheriff is siccing the Feds on me."

Jamie ignored the rude retort and said, "I'd like to come in and ask you a few questions, if you have some time."

"I already gave my statement to Finnegan," Cole said, his perfectly formed jaw tightening. "I have nothing more to add."

She didn't feel insulted by the rejection. Finn had warned her that Cole might not be cooperative. Nevertheless, Jamie was determined to win the guy's trust. When Finn had called her last night and asked if she would be willing to come to Serenade to help him out on a case, she hadn't hesitated. She had some vacation time coming up anyway—mandatory, since her supervisor believed in what he called "rejuvenating one's mind." She'd been dreading the time off, unsure of what she'd do with herself for three whole weeks, so Finn's phone call had been a godsend.

And even if she had been looking forward to the vacation, she wouldn't have been able to say no to Finn. They'd been friends for four years, ever since he'd attended a law enforcement conference in Raleigh where Jamie was giving a lecture about the art of profiling. Finn had pulled her aside after she'd left the podium, impressed by her talk and surprised by how young she'd looked. She'd shocked him even more when she'd revealed her age—twenty-eight at the time, and already with the FBI for six years. They'd ended up sharing a cup of coffee in the hotel restaurant, which sparked a friendship that had lasted all this time.

There was nothing romantic between her and Finn, never had been. They were like brother and sister, and she considered him her best friend, which was why she'd offered to help him out. Besides, she couldn't deny that this case was extremely intriguing. Heck, any case that warranted the headline *Real Estate Mogul Implicated in Death of Ex-Wife!* in the *Raleigh Tribune* was bound to be juicy. It had an exclamation mark and everything.

"I wish you'd reconsider, Mr. Donovan." She gave him a wry look. "I have a feeling you'll find me a lot easier to talk to than Sheriff Finnegan."

She could swear the corner of his mouth lifted in a brief half smile. "You've got that right."

"Please," Jamie added, an imploring note to her voice. "Just give me a half hour. Unlike many of my colleagues, I'm able to keep an open mind. I'm not here to railroad you. I just want to hear your side of the story."

He shifted, looking hesitant, but she knew she'd reeled him in. And she hadn't been lying, either. She *did* have an open mind, unlike Finn, who was pretty much convinced of Donovan's guilt. But Jamie wasn't so sure. What she knew of Cole Donovan didn't point to him being a murderer. He was only thirty-four, and already a multimillionaire. Although he'd been an heir to his father's very successful software empire, Cole had apparently chosen to donate his entire inheritance to charity and build his own empire from the ground up. Admirable, some might say.

And sure, wealthy and important men committed crimes all the time, but Jamie wasn't getting the killer vibe from Cole Donovan.

She hid a smile as he finally capitulated. Opening the door wider, he gestured for her to come inside. She took a moment to admire the interior of the house, which was made up of exposed wood and limestone, with natural wood beams and high ceilings that made her feel tiny in comparison. She sneaked a peek into a doorway to the left and saw a massive living area with a huge bay window overlooking the front yard. Oh yeah, this man was definitely wealthy. On Jamie's salary, it would take several lifetimes to afford a place like this.

"I wasn't aware the police department is working with the Feds," Cole said as he led her down a wide, wood-paneled hallway.

Jamie was momentarily startled when they entered a large, country-style kitchen. She took in the cedar counters, mahogany cupboards and sunny yellow walls, then found herself smiling at the green-and-yellow checkered curtains hanging at the window that faced the backyard. Somehow she'd expected a more…sterile environment, seeing as this man was richer than King Midas.

"This is really cozy," she remarked, not bothering to hide her surprise. "And the appliances actually look like they've been used."

"I like to cook," he said gruffly. He nodded toward the

oval cedar table across the room. "Sit down. Would you like some coffee?"

"Sure," she said as she made herself comfortable on one of the tall-backed chairs.

"Cream and sugar?"

"Black." She paused. "And to answer your question, I'm not here in an official capacity."

She neglected to mention that she wasn't technically a field agent, either. Her main purpose here was to come up with a profile of the person who'd killed Teresa Donovan, but she got the feeling Cole wouldn't appreciate having his psyche poked at by a trained psychologist.

As a profiler with the Bureau's Behavioral Analysis Unit, she spent most of her days examining case files and thinking like a killer. Offender profiling was a lot more difficult than television shows let on. It was slow, methodical work, focusing on the analysis of the offense, mainly the choices a certain perpetrator made before, during and after said offense.

Jamie looked at all aspects of the crime, from what may have triggered it, to the method in which it was carried out, to the disposal of the body. In this case she didn't have much to go on, save for the bare details Finn had provided her.

She watched as Cole moved around the kitchen, getting two ceramic mugs from the cupboard then starting the coffeemaker. Turning around, he met her eyes warily. "Then why are you here?"

"Finn asked me to come. Unofficially," she added. "He's not making much headway in the case, I'm afraid."

The coffeemaker clicked, and Cole lifted the pot and poured the scalding coffee into both mugs. Heading to the table, he handed her a mug, then sat down across from her. "Maybe if he stopped looking at me as his number-one suspect, he'd get somewhere," Cole said in irritation.

Jamie shrugged. "Maybe." She rested her forearms on the table and clasped her hands together. "Tell me, how did you meet your ex-wife?"

The question seemed to throw him. He'd probably expected her to open with 'Did you kill your ex-wife?' But that kind of aggressive approach was more Finn's style than hers.

"I was in town on business, two and a half years ago," he answered. "I ended up at the bar Teresa worked at, and we started talking. I…"

"You fell in love with her," she filled in. "And married her six months later."

He nodded.

Jamie took a long sip of coffee. "So why did it lead to divorce?"

"I mistook her for someone else," he said dourly.

Jamie didn't respond. She just maintained the eye contact, her expression relaxed. She'd found that in most interrogations, silence was often the best strategy. Stay quiet long enough, and the person on the other side of that table got antsy. Started spilling their guts just to fill the void. Though she hadn't expected the trick to work on a businessman as shrewd as this one, she was surprised when he continued to talk, his voice taking a faraway tone.

"What drew me to her at first," he said, rapping the fingers of one hand on the tabletop, "was her fire. Her spontaneity. She didn't care what anyone thought of her, didn't live to please anyone. She did her own thing, and to hell with anyone else. I liked that. I even admired it."

He halted, bringing his mug to his lips. "I was wrong. All those things I initially loved about her, they weren't what they seemed. It wasn't spontaneity or a lust for life—it was selfishness and greed."

"Did she marry you for your money?" Jamie asked frankly.

"I think so." He let out a ragged breath. "She loved being a millionaire's wife. And she hated that I wanted to live in Serenade, instead of taking her to Chicago or New York where she could live like a queen."

"Why *did* you stay here?"

"Because I like this town." He gave a faint smile. "I'm sure you noticed how beautiful Serenade is. But more than that, it's…a home, you know? It's a place where you raise your kids, where everyone knows your name and says hi to you when they pass you on the street. I grew up in a city of strangers. I wanted something different, once I married Teresa."

Jamie found herself getting caught up in his words. She understood exactly where he was coming from. The oppressive trailer park she'd grown up in hadn't been a home. More like a prison, if anything. She'd spent the better part of her adult life trying to find her place in the world, somewhere she felt like she belonged. Hadn't found it yet, either, unless you counted the Charlotte Field Office.

Realizing she'd gotten lost in thought, she gulped down some more caffeine to kick-start her focus and said, "But your ex-wife didn't want to stay in Serenade."

"No, she wanted to travel with me, even though I told her she'd only end up sitting in hotel rooms while I did business. After the first business trip—I was only gone for two days— she became petty, childish. She began making ridiculous demands, and eventually, the affairs started."

"Affairs?"

Bitterness dripped from his tone. "Parker Smith was the only one I knew about for sure—she let his name slip during an argument. But there were others. She taunted me about them."

"But didn't reveal any names," Jamie said, leaning back in her chair with a thoughtful look.

"At that point, I didn't want to know. I just wanted to get

the hell out of that marriage. So I did. I filed for divorce and moved into this house."

"Why did you stay in town? With your marriage over, it couldn't have felt like home anymore."

"Like I said, I like it here," he answered with a shrug. "Not really sure why though, seeing as everyone in town views me as the big-city troublemaker."

Jamie ran a hand through her hair. "I like it here too," she confessed. "Weird, huh? I've only been in Serenade for an hour, but I had the same feeling when I drove in. *Home.*"

Reluctant curiosity flitted across his face. "You're a city girl then?"

"Charlotte, born and raised." She smiled. "Small towns are usually my idea of hell. Boring, quiet, judgmental."

"Right about the last one," he grumbled.

She noticed that his shoulders were more relaxed, his deep voice lacking the bite it contained before. Which meant it was time to go in for the kill.

Meeting his dark eyes, she leaned forward in her chair and said, "What happened the night Teresa died, Cole?"

Chapter 2

Cole wasn't caught off guard often, but Jamie Crawford's question succeeded in making him flustered. The sudden determination in those gorgeous violet eyes threw him for a loop, and he realized she'd played him like a fiddle. He'd let her in because, as he'd told Ian, he wanted to take care of this mess. So if this FBI agent was willing to hear what he had to say, and hear it with an open mind, then what did he have to lose?

But she'd lured him into a false sense of security. Used her easygoing smiles and the complete lack of reproach in her voice to get him to open up, and then *bam!* Threw out a curveball before he saw it coming.

He drew in a breath, swallowing the animosity rising up his throat. Fine, so he'd let down his guard and had actually been enjoying the conversation with this intelligent redhead. He quickly raised that guard back up, knowing that everything he said from this point on had to be treated with caution.

"I'm sure the sheriff filled you in on what I told him," he said, eyeing her with newfound suspicion.

"He did." She paused. "He said you admitted to getting into an argument with Teresa the night she died."

"We did."

She sighed. "You can tell me what happened, you know. I'm not going to arrest you."

He arched one dubious brow. "No?"

"I didn't even bring my handcuffs, I swear."

Cole fought a grin. The idea that she even *owned* handcuffs didn't surprise him. Jamie Crawford had tough girl written all over her. He got the feeling she was very good at her job, that she wouldn't bat an eyelash if she had to take down a suspect. Yet there was also a sense of harmony that radiated from her slender body, as if she knew exactly who she was and was completely at home in her own skin. Not even an iota of insecurity emanated from her. He found that oddly refreshing.

"I went to see her at Sully's Bar that night," he admitted. "We were due in court in a couple of weeks, and I wanted to convince her to stop contesting the prenuptial agreement. She didn't have a leg to stand on, and to be honest, the thought of going to court was a huge headache."

"I take it she didn't agree with your point of view."

"Greed always trumped common sense when it came to Teresa. I tried to reason with her, but she wouldn't listen. She yelled at me, said some things that were intended to hurt me, and when I tried to get into my truck to leave, she slapped me, then grabbed my arm."

He left out a few important details. Like the sheer rage he'd felt when Teresa yet again taunted him about her infidelities. The disgust that clamped around his throat at the mere sight of the vile woman he'd once loved.

"And then?" Jamie prompted.

"I went home." His tone was hard and even. "And I have an alibi."

"I only briefly glanced at the statement Finn faxed me this morning. It said something about running into a neighbor?"

"Joe Gideon," Cole confirmed. "He lives about half a mile east of here, in an old fishing cabin."

"Okay. So you saw Joe."

He gave another nod. "I couldn't sleep—I was still riled up over the argument with Teresa—so I went for a walk. It was around two o'clock in the morning, which is when the medical examiner claims Teresa died. I ran into Joe near the creek, we exchanged some heated words—"

"Heated?" Jamie interrupted.

"Joe Gideon isn't exactly my biggest fan." Cole sighed. "He blames me for losing his job and wife."

Jamie's tone remained utterly neutral. "Now why does he think that?"

Cole curled his fingers over the ceramic mug as he leaned back in his chair. "Did you notice the hotel at the edge of town when you were driving in?"

"Yeah…"

"That used to be Serenade's paper mill. Two years ago I bought the property, shut down the mill and built the hotel in its place. All the workers lost their jobs, including Gideon. He blames me for that."

"Do you believe it's your fault?" Jamie asked.

He shook his head. "Real estate development isn't a crime. The hotel has brought some much-needed revenue to this town and created even more jobs than the mill. But Gideon doesn't see it as a plus. He lost his job, started drinking heavily, and then his wife divorced him."

Frustration bubbled in Cole's gut. "Look, I might be to blame for Gideon losing his position at the mill, but I'm not responsible for his drinking. Apparently he was hitting the bottle long before I showed up."

"Gideon claims he never saw you that night," Jamie said bluntly.

Cole was equally blunt. "He's lying. Like I said, I ran into him by the creek. We exchanged words, and then he stalked off."

"So you maintain that he's lying to the police."

"Yes, the son of a bitch is lying." His voice came out harsher than he intended. He turned his head, willing his body to relax, the muscles in his face to loosen. Just thinking about Joe Gideon made his blood boil. He wouldn't even be in this mess if that old bastard would just tell the truth.

When Cole turned back, he saw Jamie rising from her chair. She got to her feet and said, "Okay. Well, thanks for your time."

Surprise jolted through him. "That's it?"

"For now," she replied, yet there was nothing ominous about her tone. "Let me follow up on some things, and if I need to speak to you again, I'll call ahead next time."

Cole resisted the urge to shake his head in bafflement as they left the kitchen and headed back to the front door. From the corner of his eye, he noticed that the top of Jamie's head came a couple of inches above his chin. She was a tall woman, unlike Teresa, who had to fully tilt her head to meet his eyes.

He opened the door for her, but she didn't make a move to step outside. "Thank you for speaking to me," she said.

"Will you be in town for a while?" he asked gruffly. "Helping the sheriff with the case?"

"I've got three weeks of vacation time, so yeah, I'll stick around."

He opened his mouth to say something in return, but nothing came out. For some reason, he didn't want her to leave just yet. She was the first person since Teresa's death who'd spoken to him like he was a human being instead of a cold-blooded monster.

She was also the first woman since Teresa to evoke this strange sense of longing inside of him, but he decided not to dwell on that disturbing notion. Instead, he stuck out his hand and said, "Thanks for the visit."

After a beat of hesitation, she shook his hand. Almost immediately, a current of electricity sizzled from her palm to his, making them both jump.

Well, that was strange. Though she'd taken her hand back, his fingers continued to tingle, a rush of heat moving from his palm, up his arm and circling his chest. He was just wondering if she'd felt that odd spark too, when she pinned him down with an eerily insightful look and said, "Did you kill her, Cole?"

This time he was prepared for the sneak attack. "No, I did not." He spoke slowly and evenly, hoping she could pick up on the sincerity of his words.

"Okay then" was all she said. She stepped onto the porch, gave him a careless wave and walked toward her car.

Cole stared at her retreating back, dumbfounded. Hard as it was to admit it, he'd been enjoying her company. She might be a Fed, but she had the most endearing way about her. An unnamable quality that made him feel both comfortable and comforted by her presence.

Turning away, he walked into the house and closed the door behind him. In the living room, he picked up the glass of bourbon he'd left sitting on the coffee table, slowly sank onto the couch and spent an impossibly long time thinking about Jamie Crawford's gorgeous violet eyes.

Jamie's heart was pounding as she drove down the dusty dirt road leading away from the house. What on earth just happened back there? She could still feel the imprint of Cole's touch on her palm. God, his hand had felt nice. Large, masculine, with a surprising amount of calluses. She wondered when he got the chance to work with those hands. He probably lived in a boardroom, yet the strong hands and the muscular body hinted that he didn't spend *all* his time at the office.

And the visceral wave of desire rolling through her body hinted at something too.

She was attracted to him.

Lord, how could this happen? Cole was undeniably attractive, yes, but he was also a *murder suspect!* What was wrong with her body that it couldn't recognize that?

In her ten years with the Bureau, she'd never been attracted to a suspect. Or a colleague, for that matter. She made sure to separate her personal life from her professional one. *Work is work* had always been her mantra. She'd seen too many fellow agents fall in love on a case, only to break up when the danger and adrenaline fizzled out. She'd decided years ago that she needed to find a man who was in no way related to her career.

And Cole Donovan, though he wasn't an agent, was directly related to this case. This *murder* case.

Gritting her teeth, Jamie forced every last residual drop of desire from her body and focused on driving. She had to check in with Finn and tell him about the interview, and she also wanted to give Joe Gideon a call and set up a meeting. Then she had to pore over the case files and see if she could come up with anything Finn may have missed.

Which meant she had absolutely no time to lust over a sexy millionaire. Especially one implicated in the death of his ex-wife.

Feeling calm and grounded, she slowed the SUV as she entered the heart of Serenade. As she glanced out the tinted window, she couldn't help but see the same appeal Cole had described. Serenade was definitely a place you'd want to call home. It was actually quite surreal, like the set of one of those wholesome family television shows. Main Street boasted cute little shops, including a drugstore with an honest-to-God soda fountain. The street widened and curved about half-way, showcasing a town square that featured a lovely circular fountain, curvy wrought-iron benches and flowering cherry trees that had to have been transplanted from somewhere else.

But it was the town's geography that took Jamie's breath away. The majestic Smoky Mountains loomed in the west, a filmy summer mist surrounding the peaks, and she'd driven past several dense forested areas and fields in full bloom. So different from her apartment back in Charlotte, which was located near the university campus on a street boasting the constant mill of students. Serenade had none of the bustle—it was peaceful and uncomplicated, and unbelievably pretty.

Jamie's gaze was suddenly drawn to the fountain in the town square, where a gorgeous brunette holding a baby sat on the limestone base. The baby's chubby cheeks were flushed with delight, and she was squealing as her mother sprinkled water from the fountain onto her nose.

Before Jamie could stop it, a pang of longing slid through her body.

"Not now," she muttered to herself, trying not to sigh.

She'd never believed in the concept of a biological clock, yet for some peculiar reason, she could practically hear her body ticking away the past few months. It was strange as hell. She figured she'd have children eventually, but it had never been a pressing matter. She'd spent the past ten years building her career, and her professional success made her proud. Work had always been enough for her. Until recently.

Now, each time she saw a baby, that gush of yearning hit her like a tidal wave. And she didn't even want to analyze that odd spark of sorrow she felt every night when she went to bed alone. Best leave her analytical skills to prying into the minds of killers.

Serenade's police station finally came into view, a single-story, redbrick building with a flagpole sticking out of the neat lawn out front. The American flag flapped in the late afternoon breeze, and the tall sunflowers planted along the path leading to the door swayed in that same gust. There was a small parking lot at the back of the station, and she pulled her SUV into a narrow spot, then hopped out and rounded the building.

When she walked into the station, she found herself in a small, brightly lit lobby. A plump woman with gray hair sat at the front desk, greeting Jamie with a suspicious frown.

"Can I help you?" the older woman asked in a craggy voice reserved for longtime chain smokers.

Jamie approached the desk with a smile. "I'm here to see Finn. I mean, Sheriff Finnegan."

The receptionist narrowed her eyes. "Is he expecting you?"

"Yes. Can you let him know I'm here?"

"Name?" the woman barked.

"Jamie Crawford." For the hell of it, she tossed her hair over her shoulder and added, "*Special Agent* Jamie Crawford."

That got the grumpy receptionist's attention. Immediately, she picked up the phone, pressed a button and relayed Jamie's message. A few moments later heavy footsteps thudded from the corridor tucked off to the left, and then Finn appeared.

Jamie couldn't help but grin. She hadn't seen him in nearly a year, yet he looked exactly the same. He was a big man, with broad shoulders, a thick chest and long legs. His black hair was its usual scruffy mess, curling at the collar of his white button-down shirt, and his eyes were still the darkest shade of blue she'd ever seen and as shrewd as ever.

"You lost weight," was the first thing he said, staring at her in displeasure.

"Hello to you too," she replied with a laugh. Then she crossed the tiled floor toward him and gave him a big hug.

A soft gasp sounded from the vicinity of the desk.

"Relax, Margie," Finn said, chuckling at his receptionist. "You're not witnessing anything illicit. Ms. Crawford and I are old friends."

He turned back to Jamie, giving her that gruff smile of his, which always seemed to take such a toll on him. She'd known Finn for four years, and could probably count the number of smiles she'd seen on his handsome face on one hand.

"You look tired," she remarked.

"I am tired." Resting his hand on her arm, he led her to the corridor he'd just emerged from. "Let's go to my office."

The police station was even smaller than it looked from the outside. There were three doorways in the hall—a conference room and two interrogation rooms—and then the hallway widened into the bullpen, which boasted a few desks and a counter littered with foam coffee cups and chipped mugs. Finn introduced her to a lovely young woman with dark hair—Anna Holt, one of his two deputies—and then took her into a small office tucked in the corner of the bullpen.

"Thank you for coming," he said.

Jamie set her purse on the floor and sat down on one of the plastic chairs in front of the desk. She waited until Finn settled in his chair before saying, "No problem. You know I'm happy to help."

Finn raked one large hand through his black hair. "So how did it go with Donovan? Did he do it?"

A laugh flew out of her mouth. Finn, right to the point as always. "You know I can't tell you that. I only spoke to the man for twenty minutes."

"But what's your gut telling you?"

She bit her bottom lip, trying to decide if she should tell him the truth, or what he wanted to hear.

"Jamie." He sighed. "Come on, lay it on me."

"Fine. I don't think he's your guy."

Finn's features creased with aggravation. "Oh, come on, don't tell me *that*."

"You wanted the truth." She shrugged. "My gut is saying he didn't do it."

Finn looked so dejected she decided to keep his suspect alive for a bit longer. "Remind me again of the evidence you have against Donovan," she suggested. "I didn't have a chance to go over your fax in detail."

"All circumstantial. His prints are all over the house, but he lived there, so that's expected. We found skin cells under Teresa's fingernails, which are being tested for DNA at a private lab in the city."

"Do you have a comparison sample from Donovan?"

Finn gave a grim nod. "Yep, and he submitted it willingly."

"So if the samples are a match—"

"Then he can claim his DNA got there when Teresa grabbed him in the parking lot of the bar," Finn finished. "Witnesses saw her do it during an argument."

Jamie pursed her lips together. "Okay, what else?"

"Some hair samples, which are too long to be Donovan's, and most likely belong to Teresa. Those are being tested too. And a partial fingerprint on the coffee table near where Teresa's body was found."

"Do *you* think it's Donovan?" Jamie asked point blank. "And I mean from a cop's point of view, not a resident who might not like him."

"As a cop? It sure looks like he did it. The man had the motive, that's for sure. Teresa was contesting their pre-nup, and about a month ago, she sold a tell-all article to the tabloids." Frustration seeped into his husky voice. "Does any of this help with the profile?"

Jamie decided not to remind him that coming up with a profile wasn't the same as pulling a rabbit out of a magician's hat. Instead, she went silent for a moment, her mind working over the stream of information Finn just fed into it. This case was tough to figure out, especially since she had no real sense of the killer or the victim. What made her job easier, as sad as it might be, was when the perp committed multiple offenses. Serial killers had their own unique signatures, and once you identified the signature, a profile was often quick to follow.

"This case won't have one," she mumbled to herself.

"What?"

Finn's voice jerked her from her thoughts. "A signature," she clarified. "We're assuming this is the perp's first offense, right? That he or she isn't a serial killer that decided to move to Serenade."

"Right."

"Then there won't be a noticeable signature. Which means we need to examine the MO. Most violent crimes hinge on one or both of those aspects." She paused. "Other than Cole Donovan, who else had motive to kill Teresa?"

"That's the problem. I can probably list a dozen people off the top of my head who had a run-in with her."

"Such as?" she prompted.

"One of the other waitresses at Sully's Bar, who accused Teresa of sleeping with her husband. Mr. Jensen from the gas station, who she belittled for having a lisp. Parker Smith, the man she screwed around on Cole with—she pissed Parker off pretty badly when she dumped him in front of the entire town at Martha's Diner—"

Jamie let out a low whistle. "Okay, I get the point. So obviously she wasn't Ms. Popularity."

Finn barked out a dry laugh. "Those examples were just from the past two months. Honestly, I wish she'd never come back to Serenade. Life was so damn peaceful while she was gone."

"Where did she go?" Jamie asked curiously.

"She went to Raleigh for about six months after she and Cole split up, said she was moving on to bigger and better things." He snorted. "Came back like a dog with its tail between its legs about two months ago."

"Okay." She chewed on the inside of her cheek. "Okay, I think the first thing you need to do is talk to some of these people she ticked off."

"Already on it. Max and Anna have been interviewing up a storm." Finn suddenly groaned, his blue eyes honing in on hers. "So can you help? Jesus, Jamie, I need something to go on. *Anything*. Just point me in any direction."

She could sense his quiet urgency. She knew what it was like, working a case that continued to remain unsolved. But she wasn't a miracle worker, and profiling wasn't something you could do without anything to go on.

"I'll need to see the case files," she finally said. "Including the crime scene photos. Maybe I can come up with a workable profile if I have more details."

"Done. Anything else?"

"I want to speak to Joe Gideon," she decided. "He's the only one who can back up Cole's alibi, if Cole is telling the truth. Does Gideon hate Cole enough to lie about seeing him that night?"

"Possibly. But Gideon's not budging on his story. And neither is Donovan."

"So if the encounter actually happened, then Cole is most likely innocent. And if the disgruntled neighbor is telling the truth, then Cole—"

"Shot his ex-wife in the heart to stop her from messing around with his finances."

She leaned back in the chair. "All right, so I'll see what I can get out of Gideon."

"Good luck with that. He's been interviewed four times already, twice by me, the other times by my deputies. I'm not sure you'll be able to get anything new from him."

She grinned. "You'd be surprised what people tell me. There's a reason most of the agents call me in when they're getting nowhere with a suspect. I have a sixth sense about people, you know that. And suspects always seem to spill their guts when I'm around."

He went quiet for a beat, and when he spoke, she could hear the admiration in his tone. "Did you really get the Raleigh Butcher to confess to all thirteen murders?"

"Fourteen," she corrected. "He admitted to killing his sister when he was a teenager."

"Damn."

Finn sounded impressed. Most law enforcement members were when they saw her in action in an interrogation room. She wasn't an arrogant woman, but she knew if anyone could delve into a killer's psyche and unearth its secrets, it was her. Call it a gift, or maybe a curse, but people opened up to her. Particularly violent, delusional people.

"I'll speak to Gideon tomorrow and let you know what happens," she said as she rose from the chair. "And I need those files."

Finn was already reaching into his desk drawer. He extracted a pitifully thin blue folder, rounded the desk and handed it to her. "Thanks for doing this. I know it's probably not how you wanted to spend your vacation."

She released a rueful breath. "Trust me, this will be much more exciting than anything else I could have planned."

"The only excitement I want is the kind you get from

making an arrest," Finn answered with a sullen look. "We're getting ten calls a day, demanding we get this, and I quote, evil murderer, off our streets."

Jamie tucked the folder under her arm and shot him a reassuring smile. "Well, that's why I'm here." Her jaw hardened in determination. "I'll do everything in my power to help you catch this guy, Finn. I promise you that."

Chapter 3

Jamie spent the entire evening and following morning going over the meager files Finn had given her, and by the time afternoon rolled around, she hadn't gained any insights about the case. Teresa Donovan had argued with her ex-husband in the parking lot of a bar, gone home at midnight, and two hours or so later, took a bullet to the heart.

Until the forensic results came back, there was nothing to prove that Cole Donovan had killed his ex-wife. He had the motive, sure, but Jamie still couldn't reconcile the man she'd spoken with yesterday with a cold-blooded killer. Besides, judging by Finn's notes, half the town had a motive when it came to Teresa.

By three o'clock, Jamie finally closed the case folder and left the cozy suite she was renting at Serenade's only bed-and-breakfast. Joe Gideon had agreed to meet with her at four o'clock, and since she had an hour to kill, she decided to head into the town and poke around. The townsfolk probably wouldn't want to talk to a stranger, but maybe someone would have something to offer. And if not, she could always sit in the town diner for a bit and eavesdrop.

As it turned out, she did neither of those things. After finding a parking space right on Main Street, she hopped out of the SUV, glanced at a store window and got sidetracked. She stood in front of a small art gallery, admiring a gorgeous oil painting that captured the town of Serenade so beautifully she found herself walking inside.

"Can I help you with anything?" a pleasant female voice asked.

Jamie looked over at the narrow counter by the door, surprised to find the same brunette she'd glimpsed by the fountain yesterday. Up close, the woman was even more beautiful, with the creamy pale skin of a cosmetics model, enormous liquid brown eyes, and a cupid's bow mouth that had Jamie feeling envious.

"I'm interested in the painting in the window, the one of the town," she answered. "Is it for sale?"

The brunette nodded. "It just came in last week. One of our local artists painted it, Miranda Lee. She's unbelievably talented."

"Her work is beautiful," Jamie agreed.

The woman hopped off the tall stool she was sitting on and headed over to the easel by the window. "I've got it priced at three hundred," she said over her shoulder, "but I'm sure the artist would be willing to lower the price if it's too steep for you."

"It's fine," Jamie reassured. "And I'll take it. It'll look fantastic hanging in my living room."

The brunette gave a wide smile. "Wonderful. I'll just wrap it up for you then." As she gently lifted the canvas from the easel, she shot Jamie a curious look. "You're not from around here, are you?"

Jamie laughed and gestured to her business attire. "I stick out like a sore thumb, don't I?"

"Kind of." With a smile, the brunette extended one delicate hand. "I'm Sarah Connelly, by the way. I own this place."

"Jamie Crawford," she answered as she shook Sarah's hand. "I'm in town helping out a friend. You probably know him, actually. Patrick Finnegan, the sheriff?"

It was as if a light switch had been flicked off. One moment Sarah's fair face was animated and friendly, the next, it went pale and expressionless.

"Sure, I know Finn," Sarah replied, a slight edge to her voice.

Well, okay. Definitely some history there, but Jamie knew not to push for details. She could always ask Finn about it later. From the distrustful crease marring Sarah Connelly's forehead, it was obvious the woman wasn't going to answer any personal questions.

"So I guess you're here because of Teresa Donovan," Sarah added, her motions stiff as she placed the canvas on the counter and bent down to get a roll of bubble wrap.

"I am. I'm with the FBI," Jamie admitted. "The sheriff asked for my input on the case." When Sarah didn't reply, she decided to do some fishing. Might as well, seeing as this woman seemed to know both Finn and the victim. "Were you close to Teresa?"

An incredulous laugh popped out of Sarah's mouth. She quickly cut it short, offering an apologetic look. "Sorry, I don't mean to disrespect the dead or anything. It's just that you're not going to find any female in this town who was close to that woman."

Jamie raised her eyebrows. "Who hated who?"

"Oh, it went both ways. Teresa was... Let's just say she wasn't concerned with things like wedding bands." Sarah shook her head. "In Teresa's eyes, any man was fair game, even if he was taken. The women here didn't take kindly to her throwing herself at their men."

"What about the single ones?"

Sarah shrugged. "Teresa saw them as competition. She didn't want or need friends."

"What about when she married Cole?"

"What about it?" Sarah taped up the edge of the bubble wrap, grabbed a large paper bag and gingerly slid the canvas into it. "Marriage didn't stop Teresa from going after any man she saw."

Jamie had been trying very hard not to feel sympathy for Cole, but Sarah's words brought a slight ache to her chest. Murder suspect or not, she didn't envy the man. She couldn't imagine how disgraced he must have felt, how badly his pride had been damaged knowing that his wife was not just unfaithful, but *openly* unfaithful.

But was he humiliated enough to kill her?

Her methodical brain piped up and she couldn't ignore the question it raised. When it came to motive, Cole really did have a doozy of one, didn't he?

"Let me just ring that up for you," Sarah said, moving to the cash register.

Jamie absently reached into her purse and found her wallet, wishing that she could think of Cole Donovan as just another suspect, but for some reason, each time she pictured his handsome face, her body reacted in the most irritating way.

"So did he do it?"

Sarah's wary question brought a frown to Jamie's lips. "You mean Cole?"

The other woman nodded.

"I don't know yet," Jamie replied. "What do you think?"

Sarah looked uneasy. "I'm not sure. Everyone in town is pretty much convinced of his guilt—they're ready to lock him up and throw away the key."

"And you?"

Sarah shrugged. "I wouldn't be surprised if he did it. Though I'm not sure if he should be locked up or given a parade in his name." She suddenly glanced at the window. "Speak of the devil."

Jamie followed the other woman's gaze. Almost instantly, her heart did a little somersault.

Cole was standing outside, staring right at her. With a tentative smile, he lifted one hand in a wave.

She smiled back, confused by the way her pulse sped up at the sight of him. He wore jeans again, along with a pair of black boots and a long-sleeved dark blue shirt that emphasized the ripples of his broad chest.

Damn. Why couldn't he look like a normal rich person? Designer clothes, expensive haircut, pretentious smirk. Those were the wealthy people she was accustomed to, the ones whose houses her mother used to clean. Sometimes her mom brought her along if she couldn't find a babysitter, and Jamie had grown up thinking that all rich people were evil, something her mother never failed to remind her of.

She didn't think it anymore; she knew several affluent folks who were incredibly wonderful people. But it would just be easier if Cole Donovan was like one of the wealthy jerks she'd known growing up.

Maybe then she wouldn't find him so attractive.

Trying to hide her reaction, Jamie accepted the credit card receipt Sarah handed her and scribbled her signature on the slip. "Thanks for being so candid with me," Jamie told the other woman.

"Candid is my middle name."

Jamie smiled. "Maybe we can have coffee sometime, when I take a break from the case?"

"Sure, that sounds great."

With a quick goodbye, Jamie headed for the door and

stepped out of the gallery. She made a mental note to ask Finn about Sarah Connelly, though she truly hadn't had an ulterior motive when she'd suggested coffee. With the stress of her job, making friends—or making *time* for friends—wasn't usually a viable option, and she'd actually enjoyed meeting Sarah. It might be nice having some female company as long as she was in town.

"Shopping on the job, huh?" Cole said as she came outside, eyeing the paper bag she carried.

"Killing time," she answered. "I'm meeting with your neighbor in a bit."

His expression darkened. "Will you let me know what he says?"

"I can do that." She noticed he held a shopping bag, a clear one that revealed the stack of candles and flashlights within it. "Are you planning a séance or going camping?"

His mouth quirked. "Neither. I'm just stocking up on some supplies. The weather network says there's a hurricane making its way up the coast. It probably won't make it this far inland, but that's what I thought last time, and we were without power for two days."

We. She wondered if he meant him and Teresa. She also wondered why the sight of his mouth brought a spark of heat to her belly. He really did have a nice mouth. Wide and sensual, with a surprisingly full bottom lip.

Murder suspect!

She clung to the reminder, though it only left her a little bewildered. Despite Cole's rough masculine voice and somewhat reserved demeanor, she didn't feel an ounce of fear in his presence. Not that she scared easily—she'd been in the same room with dozens of vicious killers in her career, and didn't usually feel frightened. She was always aware, though. Aware of their crimes, aware of what they were capable of, and that awareness succeeded in making her cautious. Maybe that's what troubled her about Cole, not that she didn't fear him, but that she didn't think she needed to.

"I like storms," she said, trying to keep the subject neutral.

"Somehow that doesn't surprise me."

"No?"

"You seem like the kind of woman who likes the excitement."

Their gazes locked, and there it was, that rush of heat again. Even as a girl she hadn't been one to indulge in silly crushes. Boys hadn't evoked many primal reactions in her, and when she'd felt something for someone, she'd always been guarded, wondering if the boy who showed interest in her did so because he truly liked her or because he thought she was easy since she came from a trailer park. That cautiousness had followed her into adulthood, as had the lack of carnal sexual attraction.

But *carnal* was the only word to describe her reaction to Cole. Everything about him teased her senses—his silky dark hair, the hard set of his broad shoulders, his delicious scent of spice and musk.

Okay, this definitely needed to stop.

"No, I just like the sound of thunder," she said lightly, then edged off to the side. "I should get going. Gideon is expecting me—"

"You son of a bitch!"

The shrill female cry came out of nowhere, and Jamie nearly dropped her canvas from the sheer volume of the voice. She turned in time to see a petite woman marching toward them. Toward Cole.

Jamie immediately noticed the resemblance between this woman and the photo she had of Teresa Donovan. Both women had the same pale skin, inky-black hair and gunmetal-gray eyes, only this one looked older thanks to the deep brackets around her mouth and the wrinkles at the corners of her eyes.

"You have real nerve!" the woman shrieked, her fair skin taking on an angry flush. "Walking around, *shopping,* when you should be in jail for what you've done!"

"Valerie," Cole started reluctantly.

"You murdered my sister!" Eyes blazing with hostility, she lifted her hand and sent it flying into Cole's left cheek.

Jamie winced at the sound of the fierce slap, at the way Cole's head jerked back from its force. Looking stricken, Cole took a step to the side. "I didn't kill your sister," he said in a low voice.

"Tell that to the judge!"

Jamie stifled a sigh. Several passersby had stopped and were staring openmouthed at the commotion. With Cole doing nothing to end the confrontation, Jamie moved between him and Teresa's sister, softening her tone as she looked at Valerie and said, "This really isn't the place, ma'am."

The woman's jaw dropped. She glanced from Cole to Jamie, then let out a hysterical-sounding laugh. "Already got yourself a new woman, huh, Donovan? You make me sick!"

Cole instinctively moved back, as if expecting another assault, but Valerie just stared at him with daggers in her eyes. She glowered at him for several long moments, before finally storming off.

Jamie watched her go, then turned to Cole. "Not your biggest fan, I see," she murmured.

He didn't look amused. "The feeling's mutual. Valerie Matthews is as nasty as her sister was. In fact, she raised Teresa by herself, so she probably taught her everything she knew about being a terrible person."

Jamie couldn't even argue. Valerie hadn't exactly seemed like the most stable person. She made a mental note to ask

Finn about her, and the relationship between the sisters. Had jealousy been a factor there?

"I'm sorry you had to see that," Cole said with a heavy breath, reaching up to rub his red cheek. "As you've probably figured out, I'm not the most popular guy in this town at the moment."

A silence fell over them. Jamie wanted to say a word or two of comfort, but she kept her mouth closed. She wasn't allowed to reassure this man. She was investigating him, for Pete's sake.

Evidently taking the lull as a sign of goodbye, Cole cleared his throat. "I should head home and try to fix the generator, in case that storm makes an appearance."

With an awkward goodbye, he walked off, leaving her standing by the curb. Although she'd promised herself she wasn't allowed to view Cole Donovan as anything other than a suspect, his parting sentence stayed in her mind. He was going to fix a generator. So he did work with his hands. She found herself wondering what else he did on his own. Was he involved in the actual building of any of his properties?

She shoved the questions aside, a sigh rising in her chest. She really needed to exorcise this ridiculous urge to get to know him.

Fifteen minutes later, Jamie pulled up in front of Joe Gideon's cabin, her mind on the impending interview. The structure was a far cry from Cole's luxurious house. It was nothing but a small one-story shack made of logs that seemed to be rotting in several places, with a splintered door, two boarded-up windows and a weathered porch with a gaping hole in it. Jamie carefully climbed the unstable steps and knocked on the ripped screen door, then waited.

A few seconds later, a burly man with a salt-and-pepper beard appeared in the doorway. His too-close-together brown eyes narrowed, thin lips curling into a frown as he barked, "What do you want?"

She pasted on a bright smile. "Mr. Gideon? I'm Special Agent Jamie Crawford. We spoke on the phone this morning."

"Oh, it's you. Come in, I guess."

Not the warmest of welcomes, but Jamie would take it. She followed Gideon into the house, immediately overcome by the odor of stale beer, mothballs and spoiled food. Jeez, Finn hadn't been kidding when he said Gideon's life had taken a downward spiral. Just looking at the man, she could tell he was a heavy drinker. A beer gut spilled over the waistband of his jeans and his cheeks boasted a ruddy flush that made her wonder just how much he'd already drunk today.

"You can sit wherever," he said brusquely as he flopped down into a large recliner with tattered plaid upholstery.

Jamie swallowed down her disgust and finally sat on the stained brown sofa, choosing the end that *wasn't* covered with wet newspapers and an empty carton of beer bottles.

"Do you mind if I record this?" she asked pleasantly, already pulling out the mini recorder from her purse.

Suspicion clouded his eyes. "Why?"

"Just so I make sure to get everything right when I type up your statement."

"Fine," he grumbled.

Jamie turned on the recorder and placed it on the stained coffee table. "All right, Mr. Gideon, why don't we start with what you did the morning of July 15."

As the man recited everything he'd done, throwing the phrase "Had a cold one" after each task he outlined, Jamie finally had to cut him off. "Why don't you just give me a ballpark amount of the drinks you had?"

"Ten, fifteen." He shrugged. "I have a high tolerance for the stuff."

Congratulations, she almost bit out.

"Okay, so after you finished the construction job—"

"Carpentry," he interrupted impatiently. "I was helping a buddy of mine sand some chairs."

She fought a wave of impatience of her own. "After you finished that, you came straight home?"

"Sure did."

"And you were here for the rest of the evening. Didn't leave the house until the next morning?"

"Didn't go *nowhere,*" he muttered.

"So you didn't run into Cole Donovan about a half a mile from here at around two in the morning?"

"I already said I didn't go nowhere!"

He was lying. One look at his defensive brown eyes and the now even redder cheeks, and Jamie knew that Gideon was hiding something. She wondered why Finn hadn't seen it when he'd interviewed the man.

"Why would Mr. Donovan say he saw you?" Jamie asked in a matter-of-fact tone.

Gideon rolled his eyes. "Because he's a killer, and he needs an alibi."

"You believe he killed his ex-wife then?"

"Of course he did."

"Do you have any proof of that, or is it just your own personal belief?"

His brown eyes flashed. "No, I don't got no proof. But everyone knows he did it. He attacked her outside Sully's, then followed her home to finish the job."

Jamie put on an unaffected mask, all the while marveling over how facts could get so distorted in the small-town grapevine. Eyewitnesses had grudgingly admitted to seeing *Teresa* attack *Cole.* Now it was the other way around, apparently.

The distrust coursing through her blood made it difficult

to keep a professional distance. Gideon was lying—either about his claim that he hadn't seen Cole that night, or about something else entirely. Either way, the man wasn't telling her the whole truth.

Don't push him.

She heeded the advice, relying on the instincts she'd learned to trust after ten years in law enforcement. Gideon wasn't budging on his story, not today, anyway, and forcing the subject right now would only cause him to clam up. So despite the reluctance seizing her body, she pasted a smile on her face and leaned forward to shut off the tape recorder.

"Okay, then. Thanks for your time, Mr. Gideon." Rising from the sofa, she extended a hand, trying not to cringe when Gideon's beefy hand gripped hers, his dirty fingernails digging into her palm.

"So you're sending the bastard to jail, right?" Gideon muttered as he walked her to the front door.

"We're still investigating," she corrected. "And I may want to speak with you again, if that's all right with you."

His shoulders stiffened. "Why?"

"Just in case I need some more details, you know, about Mr. Donovan's reputation around town, or to answer any other questions that arise."

"I'd be happy to help," Gideon said.

A satisfied gleam entered his eyes, and she knew she'd played her cards right. She had to make him think she needed his help to railroad Cole, which Gideon seemed intent on doing. But the defensive flicker of mistruth she'd glimpsed on his face during the interview refused to leave her mind. He'd lied to her about something.

And she was determined to find out what he was hiding.

Chapter 4

As Jamie drove away from Gideon's property, she switched on the Bluetooth nestled in her ear and instructed it to call Finn. He came on the line a second later, with an eager "Well?"

She steered the car onto the road that led back to town and said, "He didn't budge."

Finn sounded oddly triumphant. "I told you he wouldn't change his story. I guess Donovan made it all up then."

Her lips tightened. "I said Gideon didn't budge, not that he was telling the truth."

"What does that mean?"

"It means he's lying," she said with a sigh. "I think he saw Cole that night, and he's lying about it because he believes this will give him some misguided revenge. He really hates Cole."

There was a long silence, and then Finn spoke again, annoyance in his voice. "Why are you so certain Donovan isn't the killer? How can you ignore all the evidence against him?"

"What evidence?" she returned. "An alibi that I think is real. An argument with his ex-wife. An upcoming court case regarding a prenuptial agreement. It's all circumstantial, Finn. Give me hard facts. Give me the murder weapon with his fingerprints on it. Give me premeditation." She let out a breath. "You don't have a solid case against him—any lawyer will get this thrown out of court."

Finn's heavy sigh echoed in her ear. "You're right. It's not enough."

A familiar cluster of trees came into view. Jamie involuntarily eased up on the gas pedal, realizing that the turnoff onto Cole's property was up ahead. Her gaze flitted to the upcoming fork, then back on the road. Maybe she ought to stop by Cole's, just to tell him the bad news about Gideon sticking to his story.

Phones exist for a reason.

She ignored the snarky voice and found herself slowing down even more.

"Jamie, you there?"

"What? Sorry, I'm here," she said. "What did you say?"

"I said that maybe we should reinterview some of the witnesses who were at Sully's bar the night of the argument."

"Sounds like a good idea," she answered absently.

Fine, so maybe she could just call him, but wasn't this the kind of news someone would want to hear in person? She was already in the area. Wouldn't be a hassle to pop in and—

She yanked on the steering wheel at the last second, turning onto the dirt road that led to Cole's house.

"Let me give you a call later and we can talk more about the case," she chirped to Finn. "Gotta go. I'm getting another call."

She flicked off the Bluetooth before he could object, ignoring the sliver of guilt that pierced into her skin. She shouldn't have lied to Finn, but she hadn't wanted to tell him she was going to see Cole. Finn's feelings about the millionaire were no secret. He probably wouldn't even think to update Cole about any developments—or lack of—in the case.

Right, because that's why you're here, to give him an update.

She reached the tall front gate and stopped the car, trying valiantly not to question her own actions. This was a courtesy call. She was being *courteous.*

Coming here had nothing to do with the fact that her heart had done those funny little flips whenever Cole was around.

And fine, so maybe his deep voice sent shivers up her spine and his mouth fascinated her a little too much. Wasn't like she would get involved with the man. He was still a person of interest in this case, which meant that she couldn't—

A clap of thunder snapped her right out of her inner debate, making her jump. The loud boom was followed by the sound of rain slapping against the windshield.

Jamie stared out in shock. She'd been so wrapped up in thinking of reasons why she shouldn't like Cole Donovan that she'd been completely oblivious to the fact that the sky had turned an ominous shade of gray. Thick black clouds rolled in from the distance, releasing sharp drops of rain that tapped against the roof of the car.

Looked like the storm Cole had predicted was making an appearance.

Biting her bottom lip, she sat in the car and glanced over at the rustic house beyond the steel gate. The shutters were rattling, and the wind chimes hanging from the porch roof swung in the breeze. Okay, she definitely needed to leave, before the storm got worse and driving became dangerous.

She was just reaching for the gearshift when another crash

of thunder echoed from outside, a streak of white lit up the dark sky and the rain began to fall in earnest. It looked like a waterfall cascading over her car, and Jamie realized in growing dismay that there was no way she could outdrive this thing.

Cursing softly, she took a breath, rolled down the window, and pressed the intercom button on the electronic panel on the gate.

Cole's voice crackled through a moment later. "Jamie?"

She was startled for a moment, then noticed the security camera mounted on the gate and realized he was probably in front of a screen looking right at her. She winced when a blast of wind blew rain through the open car window and soaked her face.

Before she could plead for him to let her in, the gate buzzed loudly, then parted.

As she drove through it, she saw a blur of motion from the corner of her eye as something dark and furry scurried through the open gate into Cole's driveway. With the windshield wipers working furiously, it was hard to tell what it was, and then the animal darted behind a patch of trees, and she decided it was probably a squirrel. Shifting her gaze, she steered the car up the circular driveway in front of Cole's house. As the wind rocked the car, she gritted her teeth, threw open the door, then ran toward the covered porch. While she waited by the door, she stared out at the incredible display of nature with wide eyes. She had never seen anything like it. Suddenly the entire sky was almost black, while the wind shrieked like police sirens.

The door swung open to reveal Cole, a look of concern on his handsome face. "What the hell are you doing here?" he yelled over the wind.

She decided to lie rather than admit the embarrassing

truth. "I was coming back from Gideon's and the storm just hit!"

She barely had a chance to finish her sentence before chaos broke out. The rain suddenly fell harder, accompanied by another crack of lightning. As the wind howled, the trees lining the driveway swayed wildly. Several branches crashed to the ground from the force of the wind, nearly falling onto her SUV.

Jamie turned around with a look of horror, and then she was being propelled backward into Cole by a forceful gust bringing with it rain that drenched them both. Cole caught her as she stumbled, planting his hand on her hip to steady her.

"Come inside," he shouted over the din.

Another boom of thunder rolled through the sky, then a bolt of lightning that split one of the larger tree branches with a sickly crack. The heavy branch broke, crashing to the wet ground, directly behind Jamie's car.

Cole curled his fingers over her waist and urged her toward the door. "Come on, we need to get inside."

She quit gaping at the fallen tree branch and let him yank her into the hallway, where she dripped water all over the parquet floor. Her hair was stuck to her forehead and cheeks, making her look like a swamp monster. Just as she was about to comment on her wretched appearance, the lights began to flicker, then went out abruptly, shrouding the front hall in darkness.

"Well," she started awkwardly. "I have some bad news."

Cole handed Jamie a towel and tried nobly not to stare at her beaded nipples outlined by the thin cotton of the T-shirt he'd given her. They'd both been soaking wet when they'd come inside, and since he hadn't been able to fix the generator, he couldn't throw her clothes in the dryer. He'd given her a shirt and drawstring sweatpants to wear, and suddenly he regretted not covering her up in a parka or something.

The tight peaks of her nipples made his mouth go bone dry. He'd been trying to convince himself since yesterday that he wasn't attracted to Jamie Crawford, that he'd simply enjoyed having someone so open-minded listen to his story, but at this moment, he couldn't deny what he felt. With her damp hair falling down her back and curling at the ends, and those perky breasts beneath his shirt, she was undeniably beautiful.

And he was undeniably turned on.

He watched as she bent forward to towel-dry her hair, then cleared his throat. "I just made a pot of coffee before the power went out. Would you like a cup?"

"Yes," she said gratefully.

"Sit down. I'll bring it in here."

He quickly left the room, breathing deeply as he headed to the kitchen. He moved through the shadows, grabbing mugs and pouring coffee. When he brought the steaming cups into the living room a minute later, he found Jamie sitting on one of the leather couches, her skin glowing in the candlelight.

"Guess you were smart to buy those supplies," she remarked, glancing at the shining wicks of the various candles he'd placed around the room.

He joined her on the sofa, making sure to keep a respectful distance. "So Gideon is sticking to his story?" he asked, unable to stop the bitterness from entering his voice.

Her mouth dipped in a frown. "For now."

"For now?" he echoed. "Does that mean you think I'm telling the truth?"

"It means he's lying about something," she replied. "I'll probably go back in a day or two and give him another push."

"You think it will help?"

"It won't hurt," she pointed out. "Besides, I can't just leave it alone, not when I'm certain Gideon is hiding something. Trust me, Cole, if he saw you that night, I'll get him to admit it."

The moment his name left her lips, a peculiar little shiver moved up his spine. Christ. Why was he so drawn to this woman? After his disastrous marriage to Teresa, he hadn't felt any inkling to get involved with anyone again. If anything, his ex-wife's betrayal had him thinking that he was done with women for good.

And then Jamie Crawford showed up on his doorstep, and each time he looked at her, he experienced a pull of attraction. An irrational need to find out if her skin felt as soft and smooth as it looked.

"Thank you," he said. "It's nice to know that someone is actually interested in finding the truth." He scowled. "If only the sheriff were more inclined to do so."

Jamie gave a wry smile. "He really doesn't like you, you know."

"Oh, trust me. I know."

She shrugged. "I think the changes you made to this town unnerve him."

"I built a hotel," Cole said, a defensive edge creeping into his tone. "Which benefited this town, I might add."

Those violet eyes searched his face. "What made you get into real estate?"

He blinked. He still wasn't used to it, the way she changed subjects so smoothly. She was obviously quite skilled at it. Ruefully, he realized she'd probably be pretty damn good in a business negotiation.

As she waited for an answer, Cole thought about her question, then chuckled. "When an interviewer asks me that, I say it's because I like beautiful buildings and creating homes for people."

She raised one auburn eyebrow. "And the real reason?"

He grinned. "I wanted to spite my father."

"Interesting." She leaned forward to put down her mug. "I want to know more."

"My father made his living buying up companies and tearing them down." Cole set his jaw. "So I decided I'd make my living doing the opposite."

"Is it true you gave away all of his money when he died?"

"Every last penny."

And now he was even richer than his father had been, ironic as that was. When he'd closed his first nine-figure deal, he'd been tempted to look up at the sky—or perhaps down at the ground—and say to his father, *What do you think of that, old man?* Edward Donovan had spent his life chipping away at his son's confidence, constantly taunting Cole that he would never amount to anything.

Proving the old bastard wrong was the greatest triumph of Cole's life.

"Yet you managed to build something better from scratch," Jamie said, sounding impressed. "You should be proud."

"I am proud," he admitted. "It was tough, starting out. I had to beg for bank loans and I did it all on my own. Those first dozen buildings I put up, that was my sweat, blood and tears."

"You worked on the crew?"

"Oh yeah. I couldn't demand those kinds of deadlines from my guys and not join in to meet them."

"Do you still do it now?"

"Not so much anymore, someone needs to run the business, after all. But I did build the house we're sitting in."

She smiled, and something shifted in his chest. For some reason, he liked making this woman smile. Liked seeing that little twinkle of pleasure in her eyes.

"It's a great house." Then she shook her head. "But I still

can't believe you gave away your inheritance. I bet your mother wasn't happy with that decision."

"She was too drunk to notice." The confession popped out before he could stop it.

"I'm sorry to hear that," Jamie said quietly.

He gave a small shrug. "She's sober now, has been ever since my father died. Once he was gone, Mom had no reason to drink herself into oblivion."

"Your father was that bad, huh?"

"Worse," he said grimly. "He wasn't abusive, physically anyway, but he was a tyrant. He wanted a trophy wife and a child who was seen and not heard. He treated us like business associates. If I'm being honest, I don't think he felt a drop of emotion for either one of us. It was all business for him, all the time."

There was no bitterness in his voice—he'd stopped being bitter a long time ago. But it surprised him that he was sharing his life story with her. He didn't talk about his childhood with anyone. Not even Teresa. But there was just something about Jamie's perceptive lavender eyes and soothing aura that made him want to confide in her.

He fell silent, listening to the howl of the wind and the loud shuddering of the roof as the relentless rain battered against it. The large bay window overlooking the front yard revealed nothing but black, with the occasional burst of silver each time another bolt of lightning exploded from the sky. He didn't worry about the roof collapsing, though. He'd built this house with his own two hands and knew it could withstand anything Mother Nature threw at it.

Turning away from the window, he glanced back at Jamie and asked, "What about you? Bad parents, or good ones?"

"Parent, singular," she corrected. "And good, for the most part. My dad ran out on us before I was born, and my mom struggled to make ends meet." She flashed him a self-deprecating smile. "No wealthy upbringing for me."

"Wealth is overrated."

"Yeah, you really don't seem concerned with it. I mean, you live in this gorgeous house, but other than that, I get the feeling you're down-to-earth, unbothered by material things."

"You don't seem bothered by those either."

"I'm not." She tilted her head in a thoughtful pose. "I guess when you grow up in a trailer park, you learn not to take things for granted."

Somehow he couldn't picture this beautiful, refined woman hailing from a trailer park.

She must have seen the doubt in his eyes, because she let out a laugh. "Seriously, trailer park. My mom had the big, bleached-blond hair and everything. She only went back to her natural color when I graduated from the academy."

"Are you two close?"

"More or less. I don't think she understands why I chose the Bureau as my career, but she's proud of me, in her own way. She even sent me flowers after I got my first suspect to conf—" Her head jerked to the side. "Did you hear that?"

Cole went quiet, listening to the sound of the storm wreaking havoc outside. "All I hear is wind and rain."

Jamie bounded to her feet and headed for the window. "I swear I heard howling."

"The wind," he reiterated, fighting a smile.

"No, it's…" She pressed her face to the glass and peered out. "When I was driving in I saw something run into the yard—I figured it was a squirrel, but—" She gasped. "Oh no!"

"What—"

But she was already flying out of the room.

Panic thrummed inside him, propelling him into action. He hurried after her, but she'd managed to open the front door and was running out into the elements. Had she gone absolutely insane? His pulse was thrown off course when he reached the doorway and watched as a gust of wind and rain nearly knocked Jamie off her feet. She stumbled, recovered, and kept going, the T-shirt he'd given her clinging to her wet body.

Bloody hell.

Ignoring the frantic thumping of his heart, he took off after her, yelling at her only to have his voice carried away by the wind. Jamie had made it to the trees at the edge of the driveway, where the tin roof that used to be on his shed now lay in a crumbled heap of metal. He pushed forward, fighting the gusts that kept slamming him backward. Lightning whipped over his head, causing the dark sky to illuminate for one brief second before it went pitch-black again.

"Get in the house, Jamie!" he shouted fruitlessly.

He reached her just as she lifted up the metal roof lying on the grass, then swooped something into her arms. Raindrops assaulted his face, making it impossible to see what she was holding. It looked furry and wet and was letting out terrified howls.

Curling his fingers over her bare wet arm, he shoved her to his side. "We need to get inside, damn it!"

Another bolt of lightning, and then he heard a sizzling noise and pushed Jamie forward just as a branch crashed down behind them. Christ, the weatherman hadn't been kidding this time. The hurricane currently terrorizing the coast had found its way inland, manifesting as a tropical storm that seemed unbelievably out of place in the interior of the state.

They moved with the wind now, letting it propel them toward the house. By the time they staggered into the dry front hall, every inch of Cole's body was dripping wet.

"What the hell were you thinking?" he roared, his tone rivaling the furious storm outside.

"I... You didn't have to come after me," she stammered, spitting strands of soaked hair from her mouth.

"What is wrong with you?" His voice caught in his throat, an uncharacteristic vise of helplessness constricting his chest. "You could have been killed!"

"I saw—"

"I don't give a damn what you saw." He grasped both of her shoulders with his hands, vaguely aware of the squirming bundle in her arms. "That was stupid, risking your life like that."

As adrenaline and lingering panic pumped through his blood, he looked into her eyes and saw the fearful glimmer in them. Realizing he was holding onto her shoulders far too tight, he loosened his grip and let out a ragged breath. "Damn it, Jamie, you scared the crap out of me."

"I didn't mean—"

He didn't let her finish. Instead, he crushed his mouth over hers and kissed her.

Chapter 5

Jamie gasped against Cole's lips, stunned by this sudden turn of events. His lips were cold, but his tongue was warm as it prodded against the seam of her lips and demanded entry. Just as she'd been helpless to stop herself from rushing outside, she was helpless to stop this kiss. It was a desperate mashing of mouths, a complete domination as Cole's tongue thrust deep and tangled with her own.

He cupped the back of her head with one wet hand, angling for better access, kissing her so hard, so mercilessly that she sagged against him, their soaked shirts sticking together.

Something was happening inside of her. She was no longer cold, but scorching hot, flames of desire licking at her wet clothing, sizzling her skin and settling in her core. Her nipples hardened, so painfully stiff that she rubbed them against his chest to ease the dull ache.

His tongue swirled over hers and she moaned softly. Was this how kissing was supposed to make you feel? Out of control, paralyzed with pleasure? Never in her life had she experienced the burning bolts of arousal whipping through her body.

The unfamiliar sensations succeeded in bringing a jolt of panic. She pulled back at the same time Cole did, noticing that his dark gaze was focused on her hip. The hem of her shirt had ridden up, revealing the butt of the Glock tucked into her waistband.

"You're armed," he said in a flat tone.

She faltered. "Of course. I'm a federal agent."

His expression darkened, as if the reminder had sucked the passion from his body and replaced it with cold clarity. "And you're in the same house as a suspected killer." His voice went gruff. "Yeah, I get it."

Jamie felt the uncharacteristic urge to apologize, but didn't get a chance as a sharp squeak sounded from the crook of her arm. She looked down at the squirming bundle she'd rescued from the storm. It was a small terrier, with brown fur matted to his little body and liquid amber eyes gazing up at Jamie in total misery. When she'd seen those big eyes peering out from under that piece of metal outside, her heart had almost stopped.

"I had to get him," she said softly. "He was trapped. I couldn't leave him out there."

"Aw, shit," Cole muttered. "That's Elmer."

Jamie held the dog against her chest and rubbed his damp head in a soothing motion. "Elmer?"

"He belongs to Agatha Tanner, she lives up the road." Cole sighed. "I always told her she shouldn't let him out without standing outside to supervise. There are too many wild animals running around this area. It's not safe for a dog this small to be alone."

"Oh, you poor little guy," Jamie said to the trembling

animal. She patted him again, then glanced at Cole. "Do you have anything for him to eat?"

Cole lifted his shoulders in mystification. "Got some salami in the fridge, which will probably go bad if the power doesn't come back on soon. Will that do?"

"Are you hungry, Elmer?" she asked the dog. He gave a tiny whimper, which she decided to take as a yes.

In the kitchen, Jamie grabbed two small bowls from one of the cupboards, poured water into one and tossed a couple of slices of salami into the other. The wet dog immediately shoved his nose into the meat bowl and greedily devoured the salami while Jamie laughed. She looked over at Cole to see if he shared her amusement, but the expression on his face stole the breath from her lungs. Lingering heat combined with dark wariness.

The tension that had hung over them in the hallway returned, the same tension she'd been hoping would go away if she distracted them both with the cute dog.

Evidently there was no avoiding it.

Leaning an elbow against the counter, Jamie swallowed. "Listen, I always carry my weapon—"

"I get it," he cut in. "You're a cop. You carry a gun."

He didn't sound upset by it, but she couldn't stop thinking about the look on his face when he'd seen her gun. She knew she had no reason to apologize, but *I'm sorry* tickled the tip of her tongue.

Cole spoke before she could voice the words. "I don't know why I was so surprised," he said roughly. "I guess…we were having coffee in the living room and I forgot about why you came to town…rather stupid of me, huh?"

"I forgot too," she confessed.

And what a thing to forget. Cole was a suspect in his ex-wife's murder. Jamie was supposed to be investigating him.

How could those little facts slip her mind? How could she have let him *kiss* her?

"The kiss…" She took a breath. "I can't get involved with you, Cole. It wouldn't be appropriate."

His gaze dropped to her waist, to the bulge beneath her shirt. "You're right," he said with a tense look.

"Your ex-wife was murdered," she added. "Whether you're cleared of the crime or not, you're still a part of this case."

She wondered if he heard the wobble in her voice. Hopefully the torrential downpour outside covered it up. She meant every word she said, though. She *couldn't* get involved with this man. It went against every professional ethic she possessed.

"You don't have to say anything else," Cole answered, his deep voice pulling her from her thoughts. "I don't want to get involved either."

She couldn't stop a prickle of offense. "You don't?"

"My marriage just fell apart like a damn game of Jenga." His chest rose as he inhaled an unsteady breath. "I'm attracted to you, but the last thing I want right now is to jump into anything new."

He was attracted to her. An unwanted thrill which only made her head spin shot up her spine at the confession. Joy and disappointment and relief mingled in her belly, forming a cocktail of confusion. She'd just said she couldn't be with him and he'd agreed with her, so what was there to be disappointed about?

And why had her pulse kicked up several notches when he admitted his attraction?

"Yeah," she finally said. "Neither of us is in the place to start something up. My job, your marriage…not a great combination."

"Right," he said with a nod of concurrence.

"So it's settled then."

"Settled."

"That kiss was a dumb idea."

Something flickered in his eyes. "Terrible idea," he agreed.

Their gazes held, and she attempted to keep her expression as blank as the one he displayed at her. God, she hated games. There was no doubt in her mind that he'd been just as blown away by that kiss as she had. But maybe it was best to pretend it hadn't shattered either of their worlds.

And it was certainly best to ignore the appealing picture he painted at the moment, with his wet shirt emphasizing every sinewy muscle on broad chest, the razor stubble gracing his strong jaw, the way his dark hair gleamed in the candlelight.

She hastily turned to look at Elmer, who'd finished eating and was now staring up at her with curious eyes. "Uh, I guess I'll turn in. Is there a bedroom I can sleep in?"

"It's eight o'clock," Cole said with the amused twitch of his jaw. "Maybe you should have some dinner first."

Dinner? With him? Sitting at the same table, fighting each little spark of desire that ignited her belly from his mere proximity?

Then her stomach gave a little growl, and she realized it was probably a good idea to eat something. She hadn't had a single bite since the morning and she couldn't sleep on an empty stomach.

"You're right," she conceded. "We should have some dinner."

He was already heading to the fridge. "I've got some leftover Chinese food from yesterday. We won't be able to heat it up, but I like it better cold anyway."

"Me too," she admitted.

She couldn't help but ogle the way the muscles of his back bunched and flexed as he bent into the fridge to pull out several white food cartons. Without those sexy black eyes on her, she drew in a calming breath and ordered herself to keep it together. So what if she hadn't felt an attraction this strong to a man before?

If Cole could waltz around the kitchen pretending their kiss hadn't affected him, then so could she.

Cole didn't sleep a wink that night, and it wasn't the sound of the rain battering the house or the roof's moans of protest each time the wind hit it. His insomnia had been the direct result of the woman in the next bedroom.

The woman who needed a gun on hand in order to be in the same room as him.

As he'd lain in bed and stared up at the ceiling, he'd choked down the bitterness that coated his throat, and forced himself not to dwell on it. He didn't blame Jamie for being cautious. Everyone else in town believed that he was a killer—so why wouldn't the federal agent who'd come here to solve the case?

Still, it grated, knowing that the lighthearted conversation in the living room hadn't been completely genuine. It wasn't about a man and a woman getting to know each other. They were a cop and a murder suspect. Definitely not the foundation for a love connection.

Besides, he had no intention of getting involved with Jamie, no matter how much the kiss had affected him. In that moment, he'd been so grateful that she hadn't been hurt in the storm that he'd given in to the reckless desire he felt for her. But her gun had been the kick in the ass he needed, a reminder of why he couldn't be with her. With anyone.

During the night, he'd kept going back to the day he'd met Teresa, the thrill that had shot up his spine as the raven-haired beauty had approached his table, her lips curved in a teasing smile. How different his life would be if he'd simply stood up and walked out of that bar. Instead, he'd allowed himself to tumble headfirst into an uncharacteristic whirlwind affair, letting his lust for Teresa Matthews cloud all common sense.

Why hadn't he seen how wicked she was? Picked up on the toxic thread winding through her body?

Stupid fool that he was, he'd married the woman. And she'd poisoned him. Infected every inch of his life, to the point that he wasn't sure he trusted his own judgment anymore.

Jamie Crawford wasn't Teresa. He knew that. He *saw* it, from the perception exuded by her gorgeous violet eyes to the determination she displayed about this case. But he wasn't going to jump headfirst into anything again. Or ever. Hell, just the notion of lowering the shield around his heart and letting another woman in made his palms grow damp.

By the time seven o'clock rolled around, he gave up on the illusion of sleep and climbed out from between the black silk sheets in his king-size bed. Outside, the storm had evidently moved on, leaving nothing but silence in its wake. And destruction, he noted in chagrin when he stared out the bedroom window at the front yard.

Tree branches littered the dew-covered grass and the shed at the edge of the driveway was all but gone. Wonderful. Three weeks ago, he'd spent four days building the damn thing and now his hard work was in tatters. He spotted the tin roof lying by Jamie's car, inches from the thick tree trunk that had collided with the ground. The sun was a bright yellow ball in a clear blue sky, the heat of it warming Cole's bare chest right through the windowpane. Looking at the cloudless sky, it was hard to imagine that a tropical storm had terrorized the town only hours ago.

After pulling a T-shirt over his head and slipping into a pair of gray sweatpants, he made his way downstairs, pleased to see that the power had come back on. The sheriff must have had the electric company up at the break of dawn.

Cole was just pouring himself a cup of coffee when he heard a canine yip and then Elmer bounded into the kitchen, his little paws slapping against the tiled floor. Jamie appeared a moment later, looking sleepy as she watched the small dog come to an excited halt in front of the food bowl they'd given him last night.

"Morning," she murmured. "Mind if I give our tiny friend the rest of the salami?"

"Go for it. Coffee?"

"Yes, please."

Cole busied himself with pouring the steaming hot liquid into a mug, but from the corner of his eye he couldn't help but admire the tall, slender woman moving around his kitchen. She wore the black pants and dark blue collared shirt she'd donned yesterday, and the clothing still looked a little damp. Her hair had a slight wave to it too, as it hung down her back, the deep auburn tresses gleaming from the morning sunshine streaming into the kitchen.

She was an incredibly beautiful woman, even when tired and rumpled. His body tightened with arousal just looking at her. And his mind was anxious for more details about her. It troubled him that he wanted to know everything about Jamie Crawford. He knew she'd grown up poor, but there was so much more left to discover. Like why she'd joined the FBI, what she did in her spare time, her favorite movies.

What she would look like naked and moaning as he made love to her…

He nearly choked on his coffee. Man, definitely not the right train of thought. Hadn't he just decided that getting involved with this woman—with any woman—was a bad idea?

"Do you want me to drop Elmer off to his owner or will you?" Jamie asked as she sipped her drink, oblivious to the inappropriate thoughts running rampant in his head.

"I'll do it when I go for a run."

Her eyes twinkled. "You run?"

"Every morning," he confirmed.

"Me too. It's part of my routine—coffee, toast, a run and then work."

"Maybe we could go running together while you're here."

The suggestion slipped out before he could stop it, and he regretted it immediately, especially when a flicker of reluctance crept into her lavender eyes. She didn't want to get involved either, he had to remind himself. She'd told him so last night.

"Yeah, maybe," she said noncommittally in reply to his offer. "If there's time."

Her words reminded him that she still had a murder case she was helping the sheriff solve, which made him think of his ex-wife again, and with that, his body stiffened, and this time it wasn't from desire.

"Will you keep me posted on any progress you make?" he asked roughly.

"I'll try." She took a long swallow of coffee and shot him a tired look. "Let's just hope there's progress to be made."

She hesitated as if she wanted to say more, and Cole crossed his arms over his chest. "What is it?"

"At some point, we'll need to discuss your ex-wife's affairs. I'm going to need more details."

Pride tensed his jaw. "I told you everything I know about that. Parker Smith is the only one whose name she mentioned."

Jamie put down her mug and bridged the distance between them, gently putting a hand on his arm. An instantaneous burst of heat seared through him.

"I know it's uncomfortable to talk about, but anything you know about the affairs will help."

He studied her face. "You think one of Teresa's lovers may have killed her?"

"It's a possibility." She made a face. "Though apparently

there was no limit to who she pissed off, so at this point, anyone and everyone is a possibility."

He gave a derisive snort and was about to respond when the keypad by the back door buzzed, indicating that the gate had been disabled. Since Ian was the only other person who had the security codes, Cole wasn't surprised when a few moments later footsteps sounded from the hallway and Ian called, "Cole? You awake?"

"In here," he called back.

Ian appeared in the doorway, holding a black leather briefcase in one hand. "Morning, boss. I just flew in to—" He suddenly noticed Jamie. "Oh. Hello."

"Ian, this is Special Agent Jamie Crawford," Cole introduced. "She's helping the sheriff with the case. Jamie, this is my assistant, Ian."

Extending a graceful hand, Jamie greeted the younger man with a smile. "It's nice to meet you."

After a moment of palpable confusion, Ian moved in for a handshake, then glanced at Cole in puzzlement. "The FBI is working the case now?"

"I'm here unofficially," Jamie explained.

At seven o'clock in the morning?

Ian's unspoken question hung in the kitchen, and Cole could see the cautious interest on Ian's face.

"I came by to speak to Cole yesterday and got caught in the storm," Jamie added.

At the mention of the storm, Ian shook his head in wonderment. "It's incredible. Some parts of town look like a war zone. The statue in the town square toppled right into the fountain and there're fallen trees everywhere. I saw a mention of the hurricane on the news last night, but didn't think it would reach Serenade."

"Well, it did," Cole said. He slanted his head. "What are you doing back so soon? You only left yesterday afternoon."

Ian held up the briefcase. "I've got the Hanson contracts for you to sign. He faxed them to the office last night, so I figured our pilot could have me here faster than it would take for a courier to get you the contracts. I knew you'd want to go over them ASAP."

"I'm surprised Hanson cut the deal so quickly," Cole said. "I appreciate your haste, Ian."

Cole's peripheral vision caught Jamie edging toward the door. "I should get going," she said, meeting his eyes. "Thanks for the shelter from the storm."

"Anytime," he said lightly.

She hesitated in the doorway. "There's the issue of the tree trunk blocking my car…"

"Shoot, right. Let us help you with that."

The trio headed outside, where Cole and Ian heaved the soaking wet tree and moved it to the side of the driveway, allowing Jamie to reverse the SUV. She gave a little wave as she drove off and Cole noticed Ian watching her with a frown.

"It can't be good, the Feds getting involved," Ian commented as they walked to the house. The British inflection crept into his voice. "The case is still all over the news, and I'm afraid the company is starting to see the effects of Teresa's death, boss."

A frown puckered his brow. "What's going on, Ian?"

They went back to the kitchen, sitting at the table as Ian slid a thick file folder in Cole's direction. "First, here are the contracts."

Cole extracted the papers from the folder and gave them a cursory glance. "Okay. What else?"

"Kendra Warner backed out of the hotel deal. She sold to George Winston."

Cole let out a curse. Winston was his biggest rival, a developer who had no qualms about poaching potential clients and no ethics when it came to business. "Did she say why?"

Ian shrugged in discomfort.

"Ian."

"She said she didn't want to do business with a murderer."

The soft-spoken revelation had Cole gritting his teeth. He'd already seen his stock take a hit thanks to the damn newspaper headline implicating him in Teresa's death, but this was considerably worse. The Warner hotel would've been a cash cow for him.

Releasing a frustrated breath, he glanced at his assistant, his expression grave. "Anything else?"

"Chicago Imperial turned down our loan application for the Lakeshore shopping plaza." Ian looked utterly miserable. "They feel you might be overextended, and that, uh, there's a chance your assets may be frozen if you're charged with a crime."

"Damn it!" Cole slammed his hand on the tabletop, sending the papers flying. He quickly collected his composure and fixed the strewn contracts.

Funny, how Teresa seemed to be doing more damage in death than she had in life. The humiliation of her infidelities he could handle, but the destruction of his business? He'd built his empire from the ground up, worked himself to the bone to become successful and now he risked losing it all.

Ian hesitated, clearing his throat. "But I do have some other news."

"Good or bad?" Cole muttered.

"You could look at it from both ways. We've had an offer for Donovan Enterprises."

His breath jammed in his throat. "What?"

"Lewis Limited wants to buy us out."

The air in his lungs slowly drained as he mulled over what Ian had said. Lewis Limited was another competitor, an outfit that had recently entered the real estate landscape and made a killing in housing developments. "I'm not selling," he grumbled. "It's ridiculous to even consider it."

When Ian didn't answer, a defensive edge laced Cole's tone. "The case will be closed soon. Teresa's killer will be caught and the public will know I'm not a murderer."

"Did your FBI agent tell you that?" There was no mistaking the dubious pitch to Ian's question.

"No, but I have confidence she'll turn up some new leads. She's smart, Ian. And good at her job, from what I can tell."

Ian's brown eyes searched Cole's face. "You like her." It was a statement, not a question.

"She's…nice."

He almost rolled his eyes. Nice? Try drop-dead gorgeous. Wildly sexy. Or maybe intelligent and captivating was a more apt description. However you described her, Cole couldn't deny that he was drawn to Jamie Crawford.

"She did seem nice," Ian conceded. Then he sighed. "But let's just hope she really is on our side, boss. The company is in trouble as long as the case remains unsolved, and if Agent Crawford is playing you, building a case behind your back while pretending to be open-minded…"

"She's not." The conviction he felt resonated in his voice.

"Like I said, let's hope." Ian's next words brought a chill to Cole's body. "Otherwise you're in danger of losing everything you worked so hard for."

After stopping at the B&B to shower and change, Jamie drove straight to the police station to see Finn, who spent twenty minutes describing to her the damage caused by the storm. He finished with, "At least I didn't have to worry about coming to rescue you. You made it back to the B&B okay, right?"

Jamie fidgeted in her seat. "Actually, I didn't. It started pouring as I was leaving, so I sought refuge at Cole Donovan's."

A beat of silence, then Finn's face turned beet red and he looked ready to explode. "Are you crazy? You should have braved the damn storm and driven home!"

A thorn of offense stung her skin. "Jeez, you really need to calm down when it comes to that man. He was a perfect gentleman, Finn."

"He's a potential murder suspect," he shot back.

"I had a gun. Not that I expected to use it, though. If he did kill his ex-wife, I highly doubt he would draw more attention to himself by hurting a federal agent." She cocked her head. "Out of curiosity, why do you dislike him so much? Don't tell me you're jealous of his wealth."

Finn barked out a laugh. "Hardly. Though he does like to flaunt his money, cocky bastard that he is."

Somehow she found that unlikely. Cole seemed unbelievably indifferent to his wealth, a huge contrast to the rich folks Jamie's mom had been forced to deal with. Kelly Ann Crawford's job at the maid company had exposed both her and her daughter to some really nasty people. Jamie's mom suffered veiled put-downs from her rich employers and had even been accused of stealing jewelry more than once. From what Jamie had seen so far, Cole didn't flaunt a thing nor did he treat her as inferior.

She suspected Finn might have some bottled-up resentment toward the guy, and his next remark confirmed her suspicions.

"When he first showed up, he bought half the inventory at the art gallery just to show everyone he could."

Jamie cast him a knowing look. "Ah, I get it now."

"Get what?" he muttered.

"I happened to meet the gallery owner yesterday." She studied his handsome face. "A stunning brunette by the name of Sarah Connelly."

Her revelation got the reaction she'd expected—the same

shuttered expression Sarah had donned when Jamie had mentioned Finn. The tight line of his jaw told her more than he probably wanted to reveal. Finn obviously had some history with the woman. Important history, seeing as he apparently hated Cole just for having had contact with Sarah.

"So you two used to date?" she added nonchalantly.

"That's none of your business."

"Did you love her?"

"Again, none of your business," he snapped.

Jamie instinctively backed off. She'd never seen this volatile side of Finn. His blue eyes had darkened to metallic cobalt and his hands had become fists, pressed tightly over the arms of his chair. She suddenly realized the question she really should have asked was *Do you still love her?* But the answer was written all over his face.

"Sorry I brought it up," she said in a quiet voice.

A breath shuddered out of his chest. "Sorry I snapped at you. Sarah...she's a touchy subject for me."

"Yeah, I see that."

As if to punctuate his statement, Finn promptly changed the topic at hand to a more pressing one. "My deputy Max interviewed a few people yesterday before the storm hit. I've got Anna typing up the statements, and I want you to look over them when you get the chance."

"No problem. Is there anyone who stands out as a suspect?"

"They all have alibis that check out, but they all share the same hatred for Teresa too."

Jamie shook her head. "What was it about that woman that made everyone hate her?"

And why did Cole marry her? she wanted to add. She kept the thought to herself. Cole must have seen something in the woman to fall in love with her, yet from everything

Jamie was learning about Teresa Donovan née Matthews, she couldn't figure out what.

"You know how I always say that some people are just born evil?" Finn gave a bleak shrug. "Well, Teresa was rotten to the core. I knew her ever since we were kids, and honestly, there was nothing good or pure about her, even back then."

"Bad childhood?"

"More or less," he confirmed. "Dad ran out on the family when Teresa was five. Her mother was a drunk, so all the responsibility of running the house and raising Teresa fell to Valerie, who's equally rotten. I think both of them felt they were entitled to something more. They had a crappy life and they wanted everyone to know it."

"Well, at least Teresa had her sister. Misery loves company, after all."

"Valerie settled down over the years. She works as an office manager for a law firm the next town over. But Teresa didn't do so well. She was waitressing at Sully's when she met Cole. Second she realized who he was, she turned up the charm and got a ring out of the deal. A few of us were tempted to tell him the kind of woman she really was, but he pissed off too many people by closing down the mill."

Finn chuckled, the sound raising Jamie's hackles. She understood the idea of small-town solidarity and all that, but these people had loathed Teresa themselves. Not one of them could have warned Cole about the woman he was about to marry? She found herself disappointed in her friend, unable to fathom how someone as honorable as Finn could let the closing of some silly paper mill relegate him to the sidelines so he could watch another man make the biggest mistake of his life.

She was about to voice her thoughts when Finn's young

deputy Anna Holt appeared in the doorway. "Got a minute, Sheriff?" the dark-haired woman asked.

Finn waved her inside. "What's up, Anna?"

Anna took a step forward, looking a tad stricken. "There's a Ronald Emerson here to see you."

"Who?"

"Ronald Emerson." Anna sounded slightly confused. "He was Teresa Donovan's divorce lawyer, and he says he has some information about the case."

"Let him in," Finn said with furrowed brows.

Uneasiness climbed up Jamie's throat, especially when Teresa's lawyer entered the sheriff's office and she saw the look on his face. Emerson was in his late fifties, a portly, bearded man who would've made a great mall Santa. Only he didn't look particularly jolly. There was a nervous flicker in his eyes, and he shifted awkwardly, as if fighting the impulse to run out the door.

Finn rose from his chair and shook the attorney's hand. "I'm Sheriff Finnegan. My deputy said you might have some information about Mrs. Donovan's murder?"

Emerson visibly swallowed. "I'm not sure if this will help in any way, but I thought I should come in."

"I'll decide if this will help. What do you have, Mr. Emerson?"

The lawyer moved toward the desk and set his briefcase atop it. Unsnapping the buckles, he opened the case and extracted several sheets of paper stapled together. Jamie noticed his hands trembled as he handed the papers to Finn.

"What's this?" Finn asked with a frown.

Emerson sighed. "The restraining order Teresa Donovan was in the process of filing prior to her death."

Jamie briefly closed her eyes. This did not bode well.

Letting out an expletive, Finn studied the older man. "Teresa was filing a TRO? Against her ex-husband?"

Emerson nodded.

"Did she say why?"

The attorney released another breath. "Because she was scared for her life."

Chapter 6

The new information sent Jamie's mind reeling. Its implications were clear. Teresa Donovan had had reason to think that Cole would hurt her. She'd even taken steps to protect herself by getting a restraining order.

This did *not* look good for Cole. And the tiny glimmer of victory in Finn's eyes told Jamie that he was now even more convinced of Cole's guilt.

So why wasn't *she* convinced?

She'd spent the entire night with the man, heard about his relationship with his parents, *kissed* him. She wasn't easily deceived, and unless Cole was the most phenomenal liar on the planet, she didn't think she'd pegged him wrong.

"Why didn't you come forward two weeks ago?" Jamie spoke up, fixing a suspicious look at Teresa's lawyer.

Emerson went a tad pale. "I was scared," he confessed. "Mr. Donovan is a very powerful man. I worried he might consider this a personal attack, and perhaps take action against me."

Jamie stifled a sigh.

"When was the order filed?" Finn asked.

"The date is on the top of the first page." Emerson rushed on. "She came to my office and admitted that she feared for her life. Apparently her ex-husband had made some threats."

Jamie raised a brow. "What kind of threats?"

"Teresa said he pulled her aside after a meeting in which we were attempting to reach a settlement. This would have been two or three days before she came to me about the restraining order. Mr. Donovan resisted the idea of settling, and left the room. Teresa went after him, and she claims he told her she didn't know what he was capable of, and that if she kept pushing him, she was going to regret it."

Although Finn's expression went triumphant again, Jamie didn't quite agree with the obvious conclusion he'd reached. It wasn't necessarily a death threat, though when taken out of context, she could see how it might sound that way.

"Are you willing to give us a signed statement of everything you've told us?" Finn asked the lawyer.

Emerson seemed reluctant, but he nodded. "I suppose I don't have a choice. If I can help put my client's murderer behind bars, then I will."

Finn moved to the window that looked out into the bullpen and signaled for Anna. When she came into the office, he gestured to Emerson and said, "Anna, will you take Mr. Emerson's statement?"

"Sure thing, boss."

"And I'll need to keep this," Finn said, holding up the paperwork. "It will have to be logged as evidence."

"I understand," Emerson said, then followed Anna out of the room.

After closing the door, Finn walked around his desk and sat down again, giving Jamie a grim look. "Well?"

Uneasiness rose inside her. "Well what?"

"This points to premeditation, Jamie. He threatened Teresa a week before her death. Scared her badly enough that she took out a TRO."

She couldn't bring herself to share in his enthusiasm. "And you don't find it suspicious that she filed the TRO two weeks before they were due in court?" She shook her head. "I don't know, Finn. This feels too calculated on her part. She knew she had no chance of breaking that prenup. She might have been trying to garner sympathy from the judge, painting Cole as a big, scary thug in order to get his money."

Finn looked utterly frazzled. "I know you don't think he did it, but you can't ignore this. Teresa admitted to being *scared* of him. He *threatened* her."

Biting on her lower lip, Jamie forced her brain into impartial mode, so she could examine the data without any bias. Her gaze drifted to the crime scene photos littering Finn's desk, zeroing in on one in particular. She found herself reaching for it, studying the macabre scene. Teresa on the floor, her black hair fanned behind her, the small bullet hole directly in her heart. Something niggled at the back of her mind and she struggled to bring it to the surface.

"Okay," she said absently, more to herself than to Finn. "Okay, this is what we know. Crime of passion."

Finn made an annoyed sound. "Yeah, I kind of figured that already."

She held up the photograph. "It wasn't an execution, or the bullet hole would be between her eyes. Our killer was enraged, he *wanted* her to die. This is where we get to see his personality.

"He's a reserved man, aloof, keeps his emotions tightly reined in," she continued. "I think he works in a distinguished position, he's held in high regard. He's a perfectionist, neat, analytical and definitely aware of crime scene procedures, though anyone could be nowadays thanks to the internet. He keeps a distance in his regular life, and as a killer, he kept that same distance. He used a gun—"

"Seems pretty up close and personal," Finn cut in.

"The opposite actually. A gun gives the killer power, but it also allows him to distance himself from the crime." She cocked her head. "What *do* we know about the gun?"

"Hasn't turned up. But the ballistics guy in Raleigh said the bullet came from a forty-five caliber semiautomatic pistol."

"Does Cole own any guns?"

"None that are registered."

"Okay. Well, back to the profile. What was I saying? Right, keeping a distance. *I didn't kill her, the gun did.*"

"That's ridiculous," Finn grumbled.

"But psychologically sound."

"Fine, even if that's true, that man you just described, reserved, aloof, emotionless—sounds a lot like Cole Donovan, doesn't it?"

"That's not who he is," she said softly.

Before she could stop it, the memory of that explosive kiss flew into her head. She remembered the unrestrained passion blazing in his eyes, how he'd taken those big strong hands and yanked her toward him.

Hoping she wasn't blushing, she said, "Cole's aloofness is a show. His emotions aren't buried deep—they're rippling beneath the surface. All they need is a trigger and they come spilling out."

"So you're saying if he killed Teresa, he would have lost control," Finn said, a skeptical glint in his eyes.

"Exactly. But this crime had an element of control. A *controlled* rage. The gun, the pristine crime scene."

Finn still looked unconvinced. "Cole could have calmed down afterwards and cleaned up the scene."

"Jeez, you really want him to be our guy, don't you, Finn?"

"He's got the strongest motive." A suspicious cloud crossed his face. "And you *don't* want him to be our guy—why is that, Jamie?"

She shifted in discomfort. "It's not about what I want. I've studied dozens of killers, I've *spoken* to them. And my instincts are telling me Cole isn't one of them."

Finn crossed his strong arms over his chest. "And mine say he did it. Especially in light of this new evidence."

"At least tell me we're going to speak to Cole about this before simply taking Ronald Emerson at his word—which is hearsay, by the way."

Finn's jaw hardened. "Not *we*. Me."

"What—"

"I want to speak to him alone. I'm beginning to think you might have a bias here, Crawford."

Disbelief flared in her gut. She couldn't believe he'd even said that. There was nobody more professional, more objective, than her, and it grated that he actually thought she couldn't remain impartial around Cole.

Was kissing him impartial?

She pushed the reminder away, but not before a rush of guilt filled her chest. Fine, so kissing Cole probably hadn't been the smartest thing to do. But it had just happened. An impulsive, crazy moment, made even crazier by the storm and the dog she'd tried to save. And so what if she might be a tiny bit attracted to Cole? She wouldn't let something as silly as desire cloud her judgment, and Finn had no right shutting her out—especially when *he'd* asked her to come to Serenade.

"You wanted my help," she said in an irritated tone. "You

begged for it. And now you don't want me along on an interview?"

He sounded equally annoyed. "I don't want you anywhere near that man, all right? It's bad enough that you spent the night in his house. You may have forgotten that he might be a killer, but I haven't. So if you still want to help, you can go over the statements Max and Anna took yesterday, and maybe take a look at the case file again."

"But I'm not allowed to speak to your main suspect," she said, bitterness in her voice.

Finn stood up. "I can handle this alone."

"Whatever you say, Sheriff."

His blue eyes were resigned. "You can't possibly be angry with me for wanting to keep you safe."

"When did I become *un*safe?"

Finn let out a sigh. "When you stopped viewing Donovan as a potential killer."

Jamie left the station a half an hour later, armed with the witness statements Finn's deputies had amassed. The plan was to find a quiet booth at the diner and do some reading, but she couldn't seem to get her thoughts in order. She didn't like arguing with Finn. He was her only friend, and yes, he was right about the evidence against Cole being overwhelming, but it was all circumstantial.

She'd worked in law enforcement for ten years, long enough to trust her gut, to heed the built-in alarm system honed by a decade of investigation. No alarms were going off, though, and her gut was insisting that Cole wasn't a killer. Were her instincts steering her in the wrong direction this time?

Or was Finn chasing the wrong man?

She smothered a sigh as she walked into the bustling diner across the street from the police station. She was in no mood to think about this case right now, or sort through her conflicting feelings about Cole. Fortunately, as she glanced around the diner, she spotted a much-needed distraction in one of the booths.

Sarah Connelly was sitting at the other end of the room, and she'd brought her baby, who sat comfortably in her mother's lap and gurgled in delight at Jamie's approach. Instantly, Jamie's heart melted. The baby had red cherubic cheeks and was wielding a plastic spoon in one chubby hand, waving it around happily. She was so darn cute Jamie wanted to yank her out of her mother's arms and run off with her.

Damn biological clock.

Jamie smiled at the infant, then glanced at Sarah. "Hi. Mind if I join you?"

With her free hand, Sarah gestured to the seat opposite her. "Go ahead."

As Jamie sank onto the vinyl red bench and tucked her purse and file folder beside her, she caught the attention of a passing waitress and ordered a cup of coffee and a BLT. As she settled in, Sarah gently took the spoon from the baby's fingers and set it on the table.

"She's adorable," Jamie commented.

A soft smile lit Sarah's face. "I know."

"What's her name?"

"Lucy." Sarah stroked the tuft of black hair on Lucy's head. "I adopted her two months ago."

Jamie glanced at her in surprise. Although her hair was far darker than Sarah's brown tresses, Lucy had the same almond-brown eyes as her mother and they were just as eerily sharp.

"She actually kind of looks like you," Jamie remarked.

"I know. It's funny, huh?" Sarah shifted the baby to her other hip and reached for her cup of tea. "So how's the case going?"

"Too early to tell. We're still waiting for the forensics results to come in. Until then, all we can do is interview folks and see if any new leads crop up."

She neglected to mention the lead that had fallen into their laps less than an hour ago. It wouldn't be appropriate discussing it with a civilian, and besides, she was trying not to think about that damn restraining order. She'd never felt the slightest twinge of peril in Cole's proximity. No fear, no apprehension. She couldn't imagine him threatening a woman, not even his ex-wife, and a part of her was extremely dubious of the claims Teresa had made to her lawyer.

"I don't envy you," Sarah said, pulling her from her thoughts. "I know Cole Donovan is under suspicion, but honestly, there are so many other people who hated that woman. You have your work cut out for you, that's for sure."

"You really weren't a fan of hers, were you?"

"Not really," Sarah answered with a shrug.

At that moment, the waitress approached the booth with Jamie's order. As she picked up half of her sandwich and took a bite, she noticed the expression on Sarah's face, as if the other woman had more to say on the subject of Teresa but wasn't sure how to raise it. She decided to do a little prodding.

"Seems like Teresa was nasty to everyone—was that the case with you?" Jamie asked between bites.

"You could say that." Lucy made a snuffling sound and Sarah stroked the baby's head again. "The day I came back to town from the city, I ran into Teresa outside the grocery store and let's just say she was at her very best. She said some callous things, you know, how I had to adopt a baby because no man wanted me." Sarah shrugged again. "She also implied she was sleeping with my ex-boyfriend."

It took all of Jamie's willpower not to gasp. Considering the pained expressions both Sarah and Finn got when Jamie had mentioned one to the other, it didn't take a genius to figure out they'd been together. Had Teresa been referring to *Finn?*

No. No way would Finn have slept with the woman.

"Did you believe her?" Jamie asked carefully.

"Not in the slightest." Sarah's next words confirmed Jamie's thoughts. "My ex wouldn't have touched that woman with a ten-foot pole. Teresa knew it, too. She just liked causing trouble, pissing people off just to make herself feel powerful or something."

As if on cue, a voice Jamie now recognized interrupted the conversation. She turned her head in time to see Valerie Matthews striding up to their booth.

"Why, hello there, Sarah," Valerie chirped. Her gray eyes landed on Lucy. "And look, you've got your baby with you. Isn't she just *adorable.*"

It was the same word Jamie had used, only coming out of Valerie's mouth, it sounded like an insult.

"Good to see you, Valerie," Sarah said in a measured tone, and she seemed to clutch her child tighter.

Valerie's black hair swung over her shoulder as she turned to face Jamie. "We weren't formally introduced yesterday. I'm Valerie Matthews."

Jamie reluctantly held out her hand to shake Valerie's. "Jamie Crawford, FBI."

Those silver eyes narrowed. "You're here to send Donovan to jail then."

"I'm here to investigate your sister's murder," she corrected.

"Then why is that son of a bitch still walking free?"

"We're gathering evidence, Ms. Matthews. These things take time."

"Gathering evidence?" Valerie smirked. "Looks to me like you're having lunch with our resident nut case."

Sarah gave a sharp intake of breath, and the raven-haired woman swiveled her head toward her. "I'm surprised you were approved during the adoption process," she said in a saccharine voice. "I assume you're taking your meds then."

Sarah's mouth set in a rigid line. "Jamie and I were in the middle of a nice lunch, Valerie. Why don't you hurry along now."

The woman looked incensed. "Don't talk to me like that, you crazy bitch," she snapped, causing several other patrons to glance in their direction.

Jamie spoke up quietly. "Ms. Matthews, I promise to keep you informed about the investigation. But now if you don't mind—"

"I do mind," Valerie cut in. "I mind very much. My little sister was *murdered* and you're just sitting here drinking your damn coffee and doing nothing to put Donovan behind bars."

"Ms. Matthews, I think—"

Valerie's eyes launched icy daggers at Jamie. "Know what *I* think? I think you're screwing him, *Ms. Crawford*. I saw the way you two were flirting on the street yesterday, and I can guarantee that whatever you think is going on with you and Cole, it's not real. The bastard is sweet-talking you so you'll forget he's a murderer."

"For God's sake, Valerie," Sarah snapped, "go cause trouble somewhere else."

"You want to talk about trouble?" Valerie replied with a harsh laugh. She glowered at Jamie. "You're going to find yourself in trouble if you let Cole swindle you. Actually, you'll find yourself dead, Ms. Crawford. Just like my sister."

Valerie's entire body vibrated with anger as she huffed off, leaving the remaining two women to exchange amazed looks.

"Wow," Jamie remarked in a low voice. "Is she always like that?"

"More or less. And now multiply that by a hundred and you've got Teresa."

"About what she said…" Jamie began.

A resigned light entered Sarah's brown eyes. "The comment about the meds?"

"Yeah, that. I know it's none of my business, but—"

"Oh, I'm sure you'll hear other people mumbling about it," Sarah said. "I…I had some issues a few years back, and…"

"You don't have to explain. I just wanted to make sure you didn't take her words to heart. She doesn't seem like a very happy woman."

"She's not." Sarah visibly swallowed. "And neither was I, back then. But everything is different now. Valerie just likes to rub salt in people's wounds. Teresa was like that too."

Jamie shook her head to herself, wondering how a town this quiet and peaceful could have produced the notorious and mean-spirited Matthews sisters. Knowing what she did about Teresa, she wasn't surprised that nobody in town seemed to be mourning the woman, not even the man who'd been married to her.

She suddenly wondered how Finn was faring with Cole, and a frown marred her mouth. She didn't appreciate the way Finn had ordered her to stay away from Cole, as if she were a silly schoolgirl rather than a trained agent.

Her appetite promptly fading, she put down her half-eaten sandwich. "I should get going," she told Sarah. "I need to read over some witness statements."

"Let's get together again while you're in town," the brunette said with a genuine smile.

"Absolutely. Why don't you give me your number and I'll call you when I get the chance."

The two women exchanged cell phone numbers and then Jamie left the diner, blinking in the afternoon sunlight. It was staggering to think that a storm had ravaged the area yesterday, what with the cloudless sky and damp humidity of the air. She made her way to the little parking lot behind the building, where she'd parked due to the lack of available spaces out front.

She froze.

A white piece of paper had been tucked under one of the windshield wipers of her SUV. It flapped ominously in the light breeze, raising Jamie's hackles. She glanced around, but the lot was deserted, and as far as she could tell, there was nobody lurking around.

As foreboding rippled through her, she walked over to the vehicle and removed the slip of paper, using only her thumb and forefinger. Even without reading it, she knew it needed to be fingerprinted. A mysterious note on her car? How harmless could *that* be?

The note had been scrawled in black ink, all capitals, and looking at it, she couldn't be sure if a male or a female had written it. But its message was undeniable.

STOP TRYING TO CLEAR HIS NAME AND PUT THE BASTARD IN JAIL. OR DO YOU HAVE A DEATH WISH, AGENT CRAWFORD?

Chapter 7

Cole stared at the security monitor, his jaw tighter than a drum as he watched the sheriff's Jeep drive off his property. He jammed a few numbers on the keypad, waited to make sure the gate was closed, then marched into the living room, each step vibrating with anger.

Before Finnegan showed up at the gate demanding to be let in, Cole had been in the process of cleaning up his front yard, hauling garbage bags of rotted branches and pieces of his shed into the back of his black pickup. Now he was too pissed off to finish the job, instead heading toward the wet bar and grabbing a bottle of Scotch. At noon. Wonderful—his drinking schedule was getting earlier and earlier. And he wasn't even using a glass this time.

A restraining order.

He still couldn't fathom it. Teresa had gotten a restraining order against him, claiming he'd threatened her life.

Did you?

Christ, he didn't even remember what he'd said to her after that meeting with their lawyers. Nothing good, he imagined, but he certainly hadn't said he was going to kill her. He'd simply wanted her to back off, give up her frivolous lawsuit and quit screwing around with him. And now whatever idiotic words he'd hurled at her were coming back to haunt him.

Now Finnegan and the D.A. could say Cole had *planned* to kill her, days before her death.

Swearing, he dropped his suddenly aching body onto the sofa and stared at the Scotch bottle in his hands. Finally, without taking a single sip, he set it on the coffee table and buried his head in his hands. He stayed in that position for so long that when his cell phone began to ring, he lifted his head to discover there was a crook in his neck.

Massaging his nape, he grabbed the phone from the table, glanced at the screen and answered with "What is it, Ian?"

"Hey, I was just calling with an update about the Hanson deal." Ian sounded concerned. "You okay?"

"No, not really," he said with a sigh.

"Did something happen?"

He put on a vague tone, not in the mood for any pity. "Nothing important. So what about Hanson?"

"Contracts are signed and we're ready to open negotiations with the contractors. Are you still set on a spring opening for the hotel?"

"Yeah, next summer at the latest."

They discussed the waterfront hotel for the next five minutes, though Cole's head wasn't in it, and it didn't take long for Ian to pick up on his boss's distracted state.

"Seriously, what's going on?" Ian demanded, cutting Cole off midsentence.

After a moment of hesitation, Cole sighed. "I just found out Teresa was filing a restraining order against me before she died."

There was a shocked silence. "Are you kidding?"

"Nope." He scowled. "Apparently she told her lawyer she was scared for her life."

"But that's...*ridiculous*." Ian paused. "The cops don't actually believe this, do they?"

"Oh, they believe it."

"Even your FBI agent?"

"She's not *my* anything, and to be honest, I have no idea what she thinks. I haven't spoken to her since she left this morning."

He suddenly wondered if the sheriff had told Jamie about the restraining order. Well, of course he had. Question was, did Jamie agree with Finnegan's preposterous premeditation theory? The mere notion that she might believe it sent a sliver of pain to his flesh. Maybe they'd both agreed that the kiss had been a mistake, but Cole still couldn't stomach the idea of Jamie Crawford thinking he was a killer. She was the first woman he'd felt a connection with since the divorce. The only woman in this town who didn't gaze at him with fear in her eyes.

"Do you want me to fly back?" Ian asked.

Cole rolled his eyes. That was always Ian's solution, to glue himself to Cole's side, as if that would magically fix everything. "No, stay in Chicago. Someone needs to make sure this business doesn't collapse."

"Fine," Ian agreed. "But if you need me to come, don't hesitate to ask."

After he'd hung up the phone, Cole reached up to rub his temples, hoping to ward off an oncoming headache. This was total insanity. Nothing seemed to be going his way. Joe Gideon refused to tell the truth and back up Cole's alibi. Teresa was taunting him from the grave with her damn restraining order. The sheriff and everyone in town wanted him behind bars. His business was suffering because of all the bad press.

How on earth had he wound up here? It was as if he'd fallen into a deep, dark hole, and every time he managed to claw his way out, someone came up and stomped on his fingers, sending him flying back into the abyss.

A buzzing sound snapped him from his dismal thoughts, then brought a rush of anger when he realized someone was at the gate. No doubt the sheriff, coming back with more questions. More accusations.

Shoulders stiff, he marched into the security room and studied the monitor, then swallowed when he recognized Jamie's car. The window was rolled down, and she was looking up at the camera, her lavender eyes flickering with the compassion he'd come to associate with her. Then her voice crackled through the speaker. "Cole? Will you let me in? I just wanted to talk."

Releasing a ragged breath, he buzzed her in and headed for the front door. As he waited, he raised his guard, refusing to be blindsided again. He doubted Jamie just wanted to *talk*. Finnegan had only left fifteen minutes ago, after Cole refused to answer any more questions without his lawyer present. And now Jamie was here, hoping to chat?

Cole's jaw tensed as he heard her footsteps on the porch. Finnegan had sent her. No doubt about that. And he had no intention of enduring another interrogation, not even from the woman who'd passionately kissed him back last night. Actually, *especially* not this woman.

To his surprise, when he opened the door and gestured for her to come inside, the first thing she said was, "Are you all right?"

He blinked in surprise. "What?"

"Are you all right?" she repeated as they headed for the living room. Her gaze flicked to the bottle of Scotch on the table, and she answered her own question with a rueful expression. "I guess not."

"What are you doing here, Jamie?" He couldn't hide the weariness in his voice, or the heaviness of his body as he trudged to the sofa and sat down.

Setting her purse on the hardwood floor, Jamie joined him on the couch. The sweet fragrance of her perfume wafted in his direction, and he suddenly noticed that she wasn't wearing the business attire she'd had on this morning. She'd changed into a pair of faded blue jeans and a black v-neck T-shirt, which made her look younger, softer.

"I was at the station when Teresa's lawyer came in," she admitted.

"So you know," he said flatly.

Jamie met his eyes. "Did you threaten her?"

Frustration roiled in his belly. "Honestly? I don't really remember. I may have told her to stop pushing me or she'd regret it, but I didn't say I was going to kill her. I just wanted to put an end to that foolish court case."

"That's what I figured," Jamie said softly. "I don't believe you meant it as a threat to her life."

He searched her face, seeing nothing but sincerity there. "You're probably the only one who thinks that," he said with a sigh. "Finnegan is convinced I'm a murderer. I'm sure the people in town think so too."

Something flickered in her expression, causing Cole to narrow his eyes. "What is it?"

"I ran into Valerie Matthews at the diner earlier," she said. "I don't know about anyone else in town, but she definitely believes you murdered her sister." Jamie paused. "I'm pretty sure she gave me a warning."

He frowned. "What do you mean?"

The frown deepened as Jamie told him about the mysterious note that had been left on her car, accusing her of having a death wish. When she finished, Cole fought a rush of anger, turning his head so she wouldn't see the volatile look in his eyes. The thought of someone going out of their way to warn Jamie about him made his stomach clench.

When had he become the villain? He'd worked damn hard to get to where he was, spent years building his business into the successful empire it was today. The only mistake he'd made was marrying Teresa Matthews. He'd let lust cloud his common sense, married a woman he'd hardly known and now he was paying the price for it.

The sympathy on Jamie's face only made it worse. He didn't want her feeling sorry for him. Didn't need her or anyone else's pity. Curling his hands into fists, he tightened his jaw and shot her a dark look.

"So someone left you a warning note and yet you still came here. What, you're not scared of me?"

She seemed wary, no doubt because of the feral expression he knew must be on his face. "No, I'm not scared of you, Cole."

"Well, maybe you should be," he muttered. "Apparently I'm the man women file restraining orders against." He cursed. "Lord, when the papers find out about this…"

"It might not get out."

He gave a derisive snort. "Of course it will get out. I'm a wealthy man and people love scandals. Know what they love even more? Kicking a man when he's down."

Her voice grew strained. "Cole, come on."

He was so overcome by a wave of atypical self-pity that he didn't even notice her move closer, not until her warm hand stroked his cheek. The gentleness of her touch only made him angrier, and with another expletive, he pushed her hand away.

"Don't," he choked out. "Don't feel sorry for me."

Her violet eyes shone with more of that sympathy he was tired of seeing. "I hate seeing you like this."

"Then leave."

He knew he was being an ass, but at the moment, he was tired of keeping up a careless front. This entire time he'd assured himself that the investigation would blow over. That Gideon would tell the truth. That a new suspect would crop up. Well, none of that had happened, and not even Jamie Crawford's soothing presence could fix his mess of a life.

"I'm not leaving," Jamie said, sounding irritated. "You're upset. You need someone to talk to. You need a friend."

He gave an incredulous laugh. "We barely know each other. And even if we did, there's no way we can be friends, Jamie."

She frowned. "Why, because I'm a cop?"

"No, because we're attracted to each other."

Her breath hitched, but she made no attempt to deny it. From the moment he'd met her, she'd triggered his desire. It was like a magnet was pulling him toward her, and that same force had him moving closer now. Everything about this woman got his blood going. The curve of her graceful neck, the flowery scent of her perfume, the way her clothes hugged her long, willowy frame.

He'd already had a taste of her, felt her lush lips pressed against his own. God help him, but he wanted another taste.

Despite the warning bells going off in his head, he dipped it, so that their lips were inches apart. Maybe if she'd pushed him away, he could have controlled the wave of need swelling in his body, but then her gaze flitted to his mouth, her eyes darkened to a smoky violet and Cole's control snapped like a rubber band.

Growling low in the back of his throat, he tangled one hand through Jamie's silky red hair and kissed her. She gasped, then parted her lips and let his tongue inside. His lungs burned from the lack of oxygen as he explored Jamie's sweet, warm mouth. His hands drifted down to grip her waist, sliding under the hem of her shirt, touching bare skin. The heat of her flesh sent his head spinning, had him kissing her deeper, harder, and as much as he wanted to keep his mouth on hers for as long as he could, he wanted her naked even more.

She must have felt the same urgency, because the next thing he knew, they were pawing at each other's clothing like reckless teenagers. Buttons snapped, zippers hissed, the soft thud of clothing hitting the hardwood floor. And then he was in nothing but a pair of black boxers, Jamie in a pale green bra and matching panties, and they tumbled back on the couch, their mouths and hands taking on minds of their own.

Cole groaned as Jamie pressed her mouth against his chest, as she lavished kisses over his feverish skin, as her hand circled his shaft and pumped him in a slow, lazy rhythm that had him seeing stars. And then she slid off the couch, got to her knees, and freed his erection. When she covered it with her mouth, the stars became a white haze that made it impossible to see, let alone think.

His head lolled to the side, too heavy to keep upright the longer she moved her tongue over him. His muscles tensed, chest tight with arousal as Jamie drove him wild with her mouth. When she rested one hand on his thigh, squeezing hard, he nearly lost control. It took every ounce of restraint he possessed to stop that rising release. Groaning, he tugged on her long hair and brought her back to the couch, his mouth finding hers once more.

This time it was his hands doing the exploring, his mouth peppering kisses over every inch of her slender body, over every curve, every secret place. He unclasped the front of her bra and his mouth went dry when her breasts spilled out, her dusky red nipples rigid and demanding attention.

Jamie sighed with pleasure as he covered one tight bud with his mouth and suckled gently. Her hands rested on the back of his head, keeping him in place, drawing him closer. As he feasted on her breasts, he tugged on her panties, scrunched them between his fingers and shoved them down her legs.

"This is crazy," she whispered, then moaned softly as his hand moved between her legs and stroked her core.

Crazy. With his heart thrashing an irregular beat in his chest and his erection throbbing relentlessly against her firm thigh, he knew she was right. Forget lust. This was something entirely different. Something carnal and out of control and—

"We can't do this," he choked out.

As Jamie blinked in confusion, Cole practically dove off her, shoving his boxers up to his hips as he struggled for breath. The sight of her gorgeous body stretched out on the couch, the trust glimmering in her eyes, her tousled hair and bee-stung lips—it all succeeded in sending a streak of guilt through his chest.

What was he *doing*? He couldn't sleep with this woman. Not with this black cloud hanging over his head, threatening to destroy him. Not while vultures circled Donovan Enterprises, watching the stock plummet and waiting for the opportune moment to snatch up the empire. He had to focus on saving his livelihood. On clearing his name. And no matter how badly he wanted Jamie Crawford, taking her would be a big mistake. He was in no shape to get involved with anyone right now. Call him a coward, but he had no intention of handing his heart over to another woman, only to have it ripped to shreds.

"Cole," she started, her voice shaky. "I—"

"I'm sorry," he cut in, breathing hard to steady his racing

heart. "That shouldn't have happened. I shouldn't have done that."

She swallowed, then sat up, fumbling with the clasp of her bra. He glimpsed a flash of disappointment in her eyes, but within seconds, it faded, replaced by the same unease plaguing his own body.

"Oh God," she whispered, suddenly jumping off the couch in search of her clothes. "You're right, we shouldn't have let that happen."

They both dressed in a hurry, as tension and lingering heat sizzled between them like an electric current. Cole was buttoning up his shirt when Jamie finally spoke. "I didn't come here for that," she stammered. "I really just wanted to make sure you were okay."

"I know," he said in a gruff voice.

"But I meant what I said about being friends. Maybe I'm being foolish, but I don't think you killed Teresa, Cole. I look into your eyes and I don't see a killer."

"Because I'm not." A lump rose in his throat. "I didn't murder my ex-wife. I can't say I'm sad that she's gone, or that I'm happy about all this so-called evidence against me, but I can promise you I had nothing to do with her death."

"I believe you."

Those three words caused his throat to tighten. Gratitude flooded every part of his body, and he found himself locking his gaze with hers. "Thank you." The lump at the back of his throat grew even bigger. "But I meant what I said before. We can't be friends, Jamie. Right now, my only concern is staying out of prison, and I can't drag anyone else down with me."

Though she looked sad, she gave a slight nod. "You were right, anyway. I'm not sure this attraction between us is conducive to a friendship."

He swept his gaze over rumpled clothing and mussed-up

hair, and a sigh lodged in his chest. "Friendship might be hard to manage."

A silence fell. Cole watched as Jamie picked up her purse from the floor and slung the strap over her shoulder. Neither of them spoke as they headed for the front door, the slow pace revealing the hesitation Cole felt, which she must be feeling as well. But it was for the best. Every cell in his body might be pleading with him to take this woman to bed, but he couldn't act on the foolish impulse.

His last relationship had died a fiery death, all thanks to him throwing caution into the wind and jumping into something without thinking. And now his life was in shambles.

Sleeping with Jamie wouldn't fix a damn thing. It would only add to his current stress levels. Yes, he knew that Jamie Crawford was nothing like his ex-wife. She wouldn't betray him. Wouldn't destroy him.

Or at least he didn't think she would.

But that sliver of doubt couldn't be ignored. Teresa had made it impossible for him to ever fully trust another woman. He refused to be played for a fool again. And if that meant staying away from Jamie Crawford, then that was something he was willing—not happy to, but *willing*—to do.

Chapter 8

Jamie's entire body was trembling as she hurried down the porch steps of Cole's house and made a beeline for her car. What had she *done?* Coming to Cole to offer support was one thing, but nearly having sex with the man? Thank God he'd stopped them before she made a huge mistake.

She slid into the driver's seat and took a calming breath, then glanced in the rearview mirror. Her reflection floored her. Tousled hair, swollen lips, a rosy glow to her cheeks.

She tore her gaze away and drew more air into her lungs. So she'd given in to her primal urges and almost slept with Cole Donovan. She'd made a mistake, and she'd always prided herself on being able to learn from her mistakes. All she had to do was recognize that sleeping with Cole would be a terrible error in judgment and make sure she didn't give in to temptation again.

Because really, what was the point in jumping into an affair with this man? Cole wasn't the man she envisioned when she thought about settling down with a husband and children. She wanted someone to balance her out, a man who was kind, stable, who'd be a good father. Someone whose job wasn't as demanding as hers. Cole was a multimillionaire real estate developer, for Pete's sake. He was probably as busy as she was, if not more so. They'd never be able to make it work.

Oh, and he was a murder suspect.

How could she forget *that* little tidbit? But for the life of her, she still couldn't bring herself to believe that Cole Donovan was a killer.

As confusion spun through her body, she started the car and placed her trembling hands on the steering wheel. She needed to get out of here. Away from this house. Away from Cole. Everything he'd said back there had been right. They couldn't get involved. And they couldn't be friends. He was a suspect, she was the cop investigating his ex-wife's death.

Then start investigating.

The annoying voice in her head gave her pause, causing her to slow the SUV as she drove through the gate on Cole's property. The image of Cole's ravaged face burned across her brain, the defeated tone of his voice as he'd spoken about kicking a man when he's down. The way he'd mocked her about being scared of him. The choked words—*"Don't feel sorry for me."*

God, she had to help him. Maybe she really was a total idiot, but she didn't like to see anyone suffer. Especially a man as strong and powerful as Cole.

Lifting her chin in resolve, she accelerated swiftly and took a left turn, not in the direction of town, but towards Joe Gideon's cabin. Gideon was the key. The one holding Cole's freedom in his hands. The man had lied to her when she'd gone to see him. He must have seen Cole that night, only he was too damn stubborn to tell the truth.

She squared her shoulders as she drove onto Gideon's

property. This time she was determined to get through to the man, to make him see that his lie was only slowing down the investigation and hindering them from finding the real killer.

Shutting off the engine, Jamie got out of the car and headed toward the disheveled porch. She knocked, waited and when Gideon opened the door with a suspicious look, Jamie flashed him a big smile. Refusing to be deterred, even when he greeted her with "You again?"

"Me again," she said in a pleasant voice. "Do you mind if I come in?"

Gideon frowned. "Is the bastard in jail yet?"

"No, but to make that happen, I need to go over your statement again."

Fiddling with the hem of his red-and-black flannel shirt, Gideon studied her for a long moment before inviting her in. "I already told you everything," he said as they headed once again into his drab, musty living room.

"I know, but I'm just here to dot some *i*'s and cross some *t*'s."

"Okay," he said warily.

They sat down on the tattered couch, and Jamie pulled the tape recorder from her purse. "This really won't take long," she assured him. "Just tell me your version of events again." She paused to offer another smile. "Every detail has to be documented for when you testify."

Gideon had been in the process of running his hand through his thick beard. Now that hand froze. "Testify?" he echoed.

Gotcha.

"Well, of course. The district attorney will subpoena you as a witness for the state. You'll be required to testify in a courtroom."

Uneasiness flickered across his face. "Court?"

Jamie tried not to roll her eyes. "If Mr. Donovan is arrested and indicted by a grand jury, he's entitled to a trial. Seeing as the alibi he provided depends on you, you will most likely be one of the state's star witnesses."

Gideon visibly gulped.

"So, let's just go over your story and—"

"What would I have to say?" he interrupted.

She smothered an incredulous laugh. "The truth, of course."

After a moment of reluctance, his bearded chin jutted out. "Fine, I'll do that."

"Okay, then let me tell you what you can expect in court, Mr. Gideon." She clasped her hands together. "You'll have to take the stand and swear on a Bible to tell the truth. Then you'll tell the judge and jury what you just told me, that you never saw Mr. Donovan the night his ex-wife died. And then Mr. Donovan's defense attorney will cross-examine you. Now I should warn you..." She let her voice drift off ominously.

"Warn me about what?" Gideon mumbled.

"Those defense lawyers...they can get pretty nasty. They'll want to discredit you, and they'll use every trick in the book to do that. They'll dig into your personal life, bring up any distasteful, well, *vices* you might have. Your entire life, your past mistakes, bad choices, all that will be brought to light."

"You don't say," he said in chagrin.

"The sheriff told me you're currently unemployed and recently divorced." She offered a sympathetic smile. "That might come up in the trial too."

Gideon went utterly silent. Jamie could see his brain working over the details she'd given it, as he weighed the pros and cons of his predicament. As angry and pathetic as this man might be, he was also proud. She could see it in the way he held his shoulders, from the tight set of his massive jaw.

He didn't want his dirty laundry aired out in a courtroom. Nobody did.

"Do you understand everything I'm saying to you?" she asked in a quiet voice.

His thick throat bobbed as he swallowed again. "I think I do, ma'am."

"Good." She unclasped her hands and placed them on her thighs, lifting her head in resolve. "So why don't we go over your story again, shall we? Tell me, what happened on July 15?"

Finn's head jerked up as Jamie strode into his office thirty minutes later. She'd caught him on his lunch break, judging from the enormous Reuben sandwich sitting on the desktop and the tall foam coffee cup. He offered a tentative smile when he saw her, but before he could speak—or perhaps apologize for the way he'd shut her out earlier—she marched up to the desk and dropped a piece of paper in front of him.

"Here you go," she said cheerfully.

Finn furrowed his brows. "What's this?"

"A signed statement from Joe Gideon, admitting that he saw Cole in the woods at 2:00 a.m. which, if I recall correctly, is when the medical examiner says Teresa died."

There was a shocked silence.

"He admitted to it?" Finn finally said, his voice laced with disbelief.

"Yep."

She didn't say another word, just sat in one of the visitors' chairs and let it sink in. Finn shook his head a few times, his shock evident, and it took some serious willpower not to gloat. She was pretty damn proud of herself as she glanced over at the lined sheet of beer-stained paper, on which she'd transcribed Gideon's revised statement.

Ah, the triumphant rush of getting the truth out of a liar.

She couldn't even credit her superior interrogation skills for this meeting. When she'd gone to see him, she hadn't had a real game plan, not until she'd seen the look on his face when she'd mentioned testifying in court.

At that moment, she'd glimpsed something that Finn and his deputies had obviously missed: embarrassment.

Poor man was mortified by the state in which he'd found his life. He might blame Cole for that state, but not enough to have an entire courtroom of people judge him. Or worse, pity him. All she'd had to do was mention what lay ahead for him if he stuck to his story, and he'd completely caved.

"I can't believe this." Finn released a mumbled curse. "Did you get it on tape?"

"Yes, and he's also willing to come in and sign a typed statement if you'd like."

Another curse.

Jamie didn't bother hiding her irritation. "You can't tell me you're angry about this, Finn. I got the truth from Gideon."

"You backed up the alibi of my top suspect," he shot back. "Hell, make that my *only* suspect."

"And that's a bad thing because…?" She gritted her teeth. "Now we can start looking in the right direction, find the real killer."

Finn stared at her in frustration. "How, exactly? We've got zero leads, Jamie. This case is at a standstill." He suddenly cocked his head. "Besides…Cole's alibi…it might not even mean anything."

She huffed out a breath. "What do you mean?"

"He could still be responsible. He could've hired someone to kill Teresa—Lord knows he has the money."

She swallowed down a rush of incredulity. "So now he hired a hit man?"

"Maybe. Or maybe he did do it himself. Time of death isn't always accurate, you know that."

"And you're developing a bad case of tunnel vision," she retorted, unable to control her irritation.

She'd gotten the truth out of Gideon, and even with that, Finn couldn't give Cole a break. He was like a dog with a bone, refusing to let it go even after he'd gnawed it all away.

"You need to accept that Cole might not be your killer. Actually, admit that he *isn't* the killer," Jamie said flatly. "It's time to look at other suspects."

"Yeah, like who? Tell me, who had a stronger motive than Cole?"

Jamie went quiet, pressing her hands on her thighs. She mulled over the question, but the frustration seeping from Finn's body found its way into her, making her head hurt. "How about Valerie Matthews?" she finally suggested. "Maybe she hated her sister for marrying a millionaire."

Finn arched a brow. "That's a bit of a stretch, don't you think?"

"She could have a motive we don't know about. And God knows that woman is a tad unstable." She suddenly remembered the note on her car, which she'd dropped off at the station with Anna before heading to Cole's house earlier. "And she wrote me a threatening note."

"Yeah, about that," Finn said. He pulled open the top drawer of his desk and removed the note, which was now in a plastic evidence baggie. "We tested it and there were no prints."

Jamie's shoulders sagged. "None? Well, Valerie could have wiped it clean before she left it on my car."

"I don't know. I'm not sure Valerie wrote this," Finn admitted, a frown pinching his lips.

"But she pretty much said those *same* words to me verbatim in the diner."

"Maybe, but this isn't really her style. Valerie is all about knee-jerk reactions. She freaks out, yells for a bit, then forgets about it. Writing a note and leaving it on a car takes thought, planning. Valerie's not a planner. Or a thinker."

"Well, if Valerie didn't leave it, then who did?"

Jamie's question hung in the room for a moment. Before either of them could attempt to answer it, Finn's cell phone went off. He lifted the phone to his ear and said, "Finnegan," then listened for a moment. "Yep, she's here…no, that's good news…I'll tell her to meet you there."

Finn hung up. "Anna's on her way to Parker Smith's house. He just got off work and agreed to another interview. You still want to sit in, right?" When she nodded, Finn reached for a pad of paper on his desk. "Let me write down the address for you."

"You're not coming along?"

"Can't. I'm meeting with the mayor in about ten minutes."

He scrawled down Smith's address and handed it to her. "Anna said she'll wait for you by the gas station near Parker's house, that way the two of you can arrive together."

"Sounds good."

She tucked the address into her purse and stood up, already heading for the door. Finn's voice stopped her before she could cross the threshold.

"Jamie…"

She glanced over her shoulder. "Yeah?"

"I'm sorry I was such an ass this morning." He had a sheepish expression on his handsome face. "If it helps, Donovan denied threatening Teresa and insisted the restraining order was just Teresa's way of trying to get money out of him."

Yeah, I know. She didn't voice the thought. Finn had no clue that she'd gone to Cole's anyway, despite his order to stay away from the man, and she wasn't about to start another argument.

"Thanks for letting me know," she said.

With a quick goodbye she left the office and crossed the bullpen toward the lobby, hoping that Finn didn't suspect she'd gone to Cole's against his order. He'd be pissed if he found out.

Not that she was pleased with her actions, either. Again she had to berate herself for losing control like that. She was thirty-two years old, yet she'd acted like a reckless teenager back at Cole's house. She'd worked so hard all of these years to be treated like a professional, and in one crazy moment, she'd nearly slept with a man who was the focal point of her investigation.

Sighing, Jamie put her inner turmoil to rest as she got into her car and typed Parker Smith's address into the GPS. She had to quit stewing over this. She'd come to Serenade to help Finn with a case, and it was time to focus on Teresa Donovan instead of mooning over Teresa's ex-husband.

Unfortunately, it was difficult not to think of Cole, especially when the route to Parker Smith's house took her right past Cole's house. She kept her foot on the gas as she passed the familiar turnoff, determined not to make another last-minute turn and get herself in trouble.

The GPS instructed a left turn and she followed the directive, reaching the top of a high slope lined by tall redwoods and flowering shrubs. She eased off the gas and moved her foot to the brake pedal, but when she applied some pressure, the car's speed didn't change.

Frowning, Jamie pressed harder. The vehicle stayed at the same pace, then picked up momentum as she barreled down the hill toward the sharp curve at the bottom.

Fighting a jolt of panic, she pumped the brakes, but yet again, nothing seemed to happen. Her heart thudded as the car hurtled toward the curve below. A hundred yards and she'd hit the turn at full speed, which would undoubtedly cause the SUV to flip over into the menacing-looking trunks of the redwood trees.

"Damn, damn, damn!"

Her hand trembled as she reached for the handbrake. She pulled it hard, praying it would stop the vehicle, but it didn't, and suddenly the nasty curve got closer and closer, and her pulse shrieked between her ears, and with terrifying clarity she realized there was only one thing she could do.

As the road came mere yards from ending and the thick tree trunks taunted her with imminent collision, she yanked on the door handle, tucked her head in her arms and launched herself out of the speeding car.

Chapter 9

While her heart raced in panic, Jamie curled at the exact right moment, the wind hissing in her ears as she flew out of the car. She somersaulted onto the grassy shoulder of the road, miraculously dodging out of the way as the car whizzed past her, tipping, as she'd expected, at the bottom of the hill. It flipped over once, twice, then crashed into a tree with a resounding metallic boom.

As she rolled her right arm bounced against the ground with a bone-jarring thud, and she clenched her teeth so hard she now tasted blood in her mouth. She saw stars for several long moments as she clutched her right arm. Gasping for air, she shook the dazed dizziness from her head and blinked wildly, orienting herself, then quickly examining her body for injuries.

Aside from the throbbing arm, her right leg ached and her body felt winded, but considering her daredevil antics, it was better than she'd expected. As far as harrowing vehicular escapes went, she knew she was pretty lucky to survive with nothing but a bruised arm.

She struggled to sit up and wiped the corner of her mouth with the back of her hand. Coppery blood poured out of the lip she'd bitten during the fall, staining the thin material of her shirt. Slowly she moved her arm, flexing a tiny bit to make sure it truly wasn't broken. Relief flooded her body when she was able to move the limb without any pain.

"Lucky girl," she muttered to herself.

Her gaze moved to the totaled SUV at the base of the slope. Well, maybe not so lucky.

"Ms. Crawford!"

She turned at the sound of the unfamiliar male voice, then fought another head rush. When her mind cleared, a wave of apprehension rose inside her belly. Joe Gideon was rushing toward her, a rifle slung over his shoulder and his eyes awash with worry.

"Are you all right?" he demanded as he reached her. "I saw you fly by me and knew something was wrong."

He knelt in front of her, his salt-and-pepper beard inches from her face. Extending a big, meaty hand, he helped her to her unsteady feet while she stared at him with growing suspicion.

"What are you doing here?" she couldn't help but ask.

"Hunting." He sounded defensive as he gestured to his rifle.

Jamie's eyes narrowed. "It's out of season."

Gideon's beefy shoulders lifted in a careless shrug. "I don't care much for rules."

Something wasn't right here. Despite the ringing in her ears and the incessant thudding of her heart, her brain was fully alert, and it told her that Joe Gideon's appearance at the accident site was more than a coincidence. He just popped out of the blue ten seconds after her brakes failed and her car flipped over like a monster truck?

"What happened?" he asked in a rough voice, his brown eyes drifting toward the car imbedded into the tree.

"My brakes weren't working." She studied his face as she spoke, but his expression revealed nothing but surprise and concern.

"When was the last time you got new brakes for that thing?"

"Two months ago," she said, her answer bringing on a fresh wave of anxiety. No way had the brakes just malfunctioned. They were brand-new.

Someone had tampered with the car.

Taking a breath, she took a step toward the road. "I need to get my purse out of the car so I can get my cell phone."

Gideon trailed after her, and the two approached the vehicle with wariness. The fuel tank looked intact, but Jamie still moved with caution. What if the damn thing exploded in their faces?

You watch too many movies.

Her eyes widened as she gawked at the damage. The driver's side of the SUV had been completely crushed, and the windshield had shattered, probably during the car's downward roll. She grew light-headed as she realized she would've been killed if she hadn't jumped out.

Ignoring the rush of fear coursing through her blood, she walked to the passenger side and opened the door, then reached in and grabbed her purse. She hastily darted away from the vehicle—those exploding cinematic gas tanks refused to leave her mind—and fished her cell phone from her purse with trembling fingers.

As she pressed the speed dial for Finn, she noticed Gideon circling the SUV in scrutiny. He bent down and peeked underneath the vehicle.

"Finnegan," a voice barked in her ear.

"Finn, it's me." She steadied her shaky voice, adding, "I hope I'm not interrupting your meeting with the mayor, but I'm afraid I had a little accident."

"What? What happened?"

"Just drove my SUV into a tree," she said, attempting to make light of the situation.

"What?"

"Well, actually, I jumped out before the tree part. Needless to say, I require a tow truck." From the corner of her eye she noticed Gideon moving to the front of the car, kneeling down again to poke his head under the mangled undercarriage.

"Where are you?" Finn demanded.

She gave him her location and he hung up without a goodbye. Tucking the phone into her purse, she glanced over at Gideon, who was walking toward her with a frown.

"What's wrong?" she asked, still unable to fight the ripples of suspicion swimming inside her.

He'd come to her rescue incredibly fast. *Conveniently* fast.

"Can't be sure, but it looks like the brake line was cut," he told her.

Her spine went rigid. "Are you sure?"

"I just said I wasn't sure. I'm no mechanic," he muttered. "Just looks that way, is all."

And he knew that because he'd peered under the car, or because he'd cut the line himself?

She took a discreet step back, grateful for the Bureau-issued Glock tucked into her purse. She didn't carry it on her person when she was off duty, but she always had it with her.

"If I were you, I'd get the sheriff to look into it," Gideon added.

No kidding. That was the first thing she planned on doing.

But Gideon wasn't done dispensing advice. "And I'd tell him to speak to Donovan first."

Jamie frowned. "Why do you say that?"

"Seems to me like someone was trying to hurt you." The man shrugged. "I think someone wants you off the case."

"You don't say," she murmured.

Without picking up on her sarcasm, he went on. "Donovan killed that woman. Don't care if I saw him in the woods. Mark my words, he killed her. And I'd bet my last dollar that he doesn't like you here snooping around."

His motives were clear. He wanted to plant some doubt in her mind about Cole, but Gideon's smirk only made her more suspicious of *him*. What if *Gideon* killed Cole's ex-wife so he could pin the murder on his enemy? What if Gideon had tampered with her car because *he* wanted her off the case?

As her mind raced with unpleasant possibilities, sirens pierced the air. A few minutes later Finn's Jeep appeared at the top of the slope, just as a blue-and-white cruiser skidded up from the other direction. Both Finn and Anna Holt arrived at the scene, each one wearing identical looks of concern.

"Are you all right?" Finn demanded as he hurried toward her.

She cradled her sore arm and nodded. "Just a little bruised up."

His blue eyes shifted to the destroyed SUV, and he let out a sharp whistle. "Jesus, Jamie, you could have been killed." Then that gaze landed on Gideon and a scowl graced Finn's mouth. "What are you doing here, Gideon?"

"I saw the accident and came to help," the man mumbled. "I was just leaving, though."

The sheriff's eyes narrowed. "Well, don't go too far, Joe. I'll send a deputy over in a bit to take a statement from you."

"Whatever you say, Sheriff."

Jamie and Finn watched Gideon amble off, his rifle swinging back and forth as he scurried off the shoulder and disappeared into the trees.

Anna Holt spoke first. "Is it just me, or do you guys think it's really suspicious that he was first on the scene?"

Jamie sighed. "It's not just you." She glanced at Finn. "He checked out the car, said the brake lines might have been cut."

Finn looked shocked. "Are you serious?"

"That's what Gideon thinks. But we should probably get a mechanic to look at it."

"That's my first priority." He shook his head. "Scratch that, it's my second priority. Right now I'm driving you to the clinic to get checked out."

She groaned in protest. "I'm fine, Finn. I don't need a doc—"

"No argument," he interrupted, a ferocious scowl on his face. "Now get in the Jeep so I can take you to the clinic."

"Jeez, Finn—"

"Get in the damn Jeep, Jamie."

"Well, it's not broken," Dr. Travis Bennett concluded, removing the X-ray he'd taken of Jamie's arm from the backlit white board. He turned with a reassuring smile, which only irked her even more.

"I knew it wasn't broken," she grumbled from her place on the narrow gurney. "I told Finn there was no reason to come to the clinic."

"Better safe than sorry," Finn grumbled back, his broad frame filling the doorway.

"The sheriff's right," Dr. Bennett agreed. "It's always prudent to get checked out after an accident." The tall man stepped to the door. "I'm going to write you up a prescription for painkillers."

"I don't need painkillers," she objected.

He simply offered an indulgent smile. "Trust me, you'll

thank me tonight, when all those scrapes and bruises start throbbing."

After the doctor left the room, Finn came inside, a frown marring his mouth. "I just got off the phone with the mechanic."

"And?"

"He did an initial examination of the SUV and confirmed what Gideon said. The brake lines were cut."

Unhappiness lodged in her chest. "Could it have happened on its own?"

Finn shook his head. "It was a clean cut. Whoever did it left about a quarter of the line intact, so that the brake fluid drained out slowly."

She furrowed her brows. "So they couldn't have known when the brakes would stop working. Which means Gideon would have to be a mind reader to know to be on that stretch of the road at the exact moment."

"Unless he was following you since you left his house, waiting for you to die."

"But when would he have tampered with my brakes? I was with him the entire time at his house."

"Did you go anywhere else?" Finn asked. "Park somewhere for a bit?"

Cole's house. She'd been at Cole's house. But she couldn't tell Finn, not when he'd ordered her to stay away from the man. Besides, she'd been with Cole the entire time too. They'd been busy...not sleeping together. No way could he have messed around with her car.

"By the way," Finn added darkly, "I walked over to the parking lot at the station and saw four puddles of fluid on the pavement."

"You did?"

"Yep. How the hell didn't you notice that, Jamie? You shouldn't have gotten into that car, damn it."

"I...I was distracted, I guess."

By Cole Donovan and his potent masculinity.

She wanted to berate herself for being so stupid, for not noticing that her car was leaking brake fluid all over the place. God, she could have *died*. And all because she hadn't been firing on all cylinders, all because her confusing feelings for Cole kept spinning around in her head like a damn carousel.

"Steve will go over the car more thoroughly, but I think it's safe to say that someone intentionally tried to hurt you," Finn said.

"I think you're right. But who?" She swallowed. "Gideon tried to imply that it was Cole."

"Did he say why?"

"He thinks Cole wanted me off the case because he doesn't like me snooping around."

Finn didn't answer.

"Come on, Finn, that's ridiculous and you know it," she shot out. "I just backed up Cole's alibi."

"But he doesn't know that. And besides, I'm not convinced the alibi even clears him," Finn replied. "Maybe Gideon's right and Cole wanted you out of the way before you got too close to the truth."

"That's ridiculous," she said again.

"Doesn't make it untrue."

"Doesn't make it true either."

They scowled at each other for a second, only turning away when an angry voice echoed from the hallway.

"Damn it, I want to see Agent Crawford."

Jamie's heart skipped a beat as she recognized the voice.

"I told you" came Dr. Bennett's muffled voice. "You can't just storm in here making demands. You are not allowed to go back there. You aren't— Mr. Donovan! You can't go back there!"

The thump of heavy footsteps sounded from the corridor

and then Cole burst through the doorway, his dark eyes immediately seeking out Jamie's.

"Are you all right?" he demanded.

The anxiety flashing across his face made her heart do another flip. She tried to ignore the rush of warmth that flooded her body. "I'm fine. Just a little scraped up."

Slowly, Cole entered the room. He looked like he wanted to take her into his arms, then thought better of it and stopped, leaning one broad shoulder against the wall. "I heard about the accident and came right over."

That earned him a hard glare from the sheriff. "And how exactly did you hear about it, Donovan? It surely wasn't on the news."

Cole glared right back. "I was getting takeout from the diner and saw Jamie's car being towed in. I went outside, noticed your Jeep parked in front of the clinic, and figured she was here."

Discomfort roiled in Jamie's stomach as the two men studied each other like two wary animals making a territorial stand. Their mutual dislike was hard to miss, and she decided to diffuse the situation before one challenged the other to duel or something.

"I wasn't in the car when it crashed," she assured Cole. "I jumped out just in time."

He looked appalled. "You jumped out? Are you crazy?"

"Watch your tone," Finn snapped, despite the fact that he'd been lecturing her about the same thing less than five minutes ago.

Cole swiveled his head at the other man. "Did someone tamper with the car?"

"Looks like it. The brake lines were cut." Finn offered a mocking smile. "How good are you with cars, Donovan?"

"Are you implying I'm to blame for this?"

"I'm not implying a damn thing."

"Like hell you aren't."

"Hey," Jamie interceded. "Both of you, just calm down." She glanced at Cole. "We're not sure what happened yet. The mechanic is going to take a closer look."

Cole didn't seem appeased as he turned to Finn once more. "What if the person who killed Teresa has Jamie in his sights now?"

When Finn snorted, Cole's jaw tensed. "That person wasn't me, damn it! No matter what you think of me, I don't want Jamie hurt."

"Neither do I," Finn relented.

"Then find out who cut those brakes, Finnegan."

"Don't tell me how to do my job."

Jamie sighed loudly. "Can you two please stop? Stop bickering so we can figure out who did this."

"That's the sheriff's job," Cole retorted. His lips tightened. "And while he does that job, I'm going to make sure you're protected."

She had to laugh. "I don't need you to protect me. I'm a federal agent."

"Tough," he said, sounding like the consummate alpha male. "You've got my protection whether you like it or not."

She laughed again.

"I'm serious, Jamie."

"Okay, and how do you propose to protect me?" she had to ask.

"I think you should stay with me until the sheriff catches whoever tried to kill you."

A deafening silence pounced on the room. Jamie tried to hide her shock, but it was difficult. A couple of hours ago he was telling her they couldn't get involved, and now he wanted her to stay at his house?

After a long moment, Finn cleared his throat. Shooting her a strange look, he said, "Jamie, can I speak to you alone?"

A breath shuddered out of her mouth. "Cole, will you excuse us for a second?"

With a nod, Cole stepped out the door, which Finn made a quick move toward so he could close it. He walked back to the gurney, stood a foot away from her and said, "What the hell is going on with you and Donovan?"

She gulped. "Nothing's going on."

"Then why is he suddenly your biggest protector?" Finn cursed. "And why the *hell* is he demanding you *stay at his house?*"

"I guess he's just trying to be nice." She winced at the feeble tremble to her voice.

"Nice?" Finn roared. "Look, I don't care if you got Gideon to back up his alibi! I don't trust the guy, and there's no way in hell I'm allowing you to have a *slumber party* with him!"

She clenched her teeth. "You're not *allowing* me to do anything. I make my own decisions, Finn. And you've got to admit, he's got a good point. His house might be the safest place in town."

Finn's face went beet red. "I can't believe you're even considering this!"

"Why not? He's got a locked gate, a top-notch alarm, cameras, motion sensors around the property. I took a peek into his security room and it was pretty impressive."

"The best security system in the world isn't going to help when it keeps you locked in with a murderer."

"He's not a murderer," she said in an even tone.

And this time there was no doubt in her mind. Maybe Finn didn't trust in Cole's alibi, but she did. In her profession she'd come across a lot of pretty awful people. She knew a bad man when she saw one, and Cole Donovan was not a bad man.

"You're not going home with him," Finn said, making a frustrated sound in the back of his throat. "I agree that you need protection, now that someone tried to bring you harm, but you can stay with me."

She crossed her arms. "At your isolated farmhouse?"

Finn's lips tightened. "Fine, then leave town. We're not making any headway with the case anyway."

She experienced a burst of irritation. "I'm not leaving Serenade until we catch this killer, Finn. You asked for my help. So guess what—you're stuck with me. And I think staying at Cole's place isn't such a bad idea."

Finn raked both hands through his black hair, then let out a string of curses that would've made her blush if she weren't so pissed off. "I can't believe this," he muttered. With a scowl he stalked toward the door, over his shoulder adding, "I swear, Jamie, if he pulls something, you'll have nobody to blame but yourself."

Finn stormed out of the room, leaving her staring at the doorway in shock. For a moment she was tempted to run after him, but she forced herself to stay put. She understood his anger stemmed from concern, that he was truly worried about her safety, but she didn't appreciate being treated like a dumb kid. She could protect herself, with or without Cole's offer to stay with him, but a good security system didn't hurt. She just wished Finn would put aside his damn dislike for Cole and see that she had nothing to fear from him.

"Uh, yeah. So I didn't mean to cause trouble between you two."

She glanced up at the sound of Cole's voice. He looked uncomfortable as he reentered the room, his dark eyes flickering apologetically.

"Finn is just being overprotective," she said with a sigh.

"I don't blame him. Someone tried to kill you today." He gave an awkward pause. "I couldn't help but overhear—Finnegan wasn't trying to be quiet about it—but...did Gideon really sign a statement backing up my story?"

"He did," she confirmed.

His handsome face lit up, stealing the breath right out of her lips. He looked even more gorgeous without that crease of worry in his forehead. And his voice was husky as he said, "Thank you for getting the truth out of him."

"My pleasure," she murmured.

They watched each other for a few seconds, and then Cole let out a breath. "I'm sorry if I was unreasonably harsh before, when I said we couldn't be friends."

"You were right," she said quietly.

"I was wrong," he corrected. "Just because we shouldn't act on this crazy attraction between us doesn't mean we can't be friends. And I really think you should stay with me until the sheriff finds the person who messed with your car."

She hesitated.

"Please," Cole added, his voice gruff. "Let me do this for you. You got the truth from Gideon, the least I can do is make sure you have a safe place to stay."

Jamie bit her lower lip, feeling her resolve crumble. His house was more secure than her room at the B&B, and though she wasn't going to say it aloud, the car accident had left her pretty shaken. Somebody had intentionally cut her brake lines. Whether her death was the ultimate goal didn't matter. She could have been seriously injured, and it troubled her to know she'd made an enemy in this town, that someone truly wanted to hurt her.

But was placing herself in close quarters with Cole a good idea? Her body continued to betray her whenever this man was around. Each time she looked into his charcoal eyes she melted. She was drawn to him, aroused by him. Yet she knew getting involved with him would be a mistake. Not only did they come from different worlds, but she was trying to solve his ex-wife's murder. She might not be working the case officially, but she had a strict code when it came to sex on the job.

Then don't have sex with him.

The nonchalant thought gave her pause. Because really, why was she assuming that staying at Cole's house automatically meant they'd sleep together? She was thirty-two years old. Surely she could muster up some self-control and keep her hands off the man.

"Okay," she finally said.

"Okay?" he echoed.

She exhaled a long breath. "I'll come home with you."

Chapter 10

This was a bad idea. The entire drive to his house, Cole kept his eyes on the road and tried not to question his motives for bringing Jamie home with him. He was just providing her with a safe house. Protecting her. It had nothing to do with the fact that whenever he was around her a rush of heat shuddered through his veins, or that the thought of falling into bed with her made his groin tighten.

Right, nothing to do with that.

But…he could no longer deny that he cared about this woman. When he'd looked out the diner window and seen Jamie's crumpled SUV being towed in, his entire body had gone paralyzed with fear. Then flooded with relief when he'd seen Jamie in the clinic, safe and sound.

It made him ill at ease, how much he cared about her well-being. Ever since the divorce, he'd vowed to stay detached, to avoid any lasting contact with the female gender. When Jamie had left his house after they'd almost made love, he'd told himself it was for the best, that he'd successfully avoided any risk of developing feelings other than desire for her. And then she went ahead and almost got killed, and now there was no way he could pretend he didn't care.

Shoving away his disconcerting thoughts, he drove through the gate and pulled into his driveway, shooting her a concerned look as he shut off the engine. "How are you feeling?" he asked.

She shrugged. "A little sore, but I was lucky to escape with only a few bruises."

"Maybe a hot bath will help. You can use the Jacuzzi in the master bedroom," he offered.

Although he'd sincerely been thinking about her aching body, the second he pictured Jamie naked in his Jacuzzi, arousal burned in his blood. Must have burned in his eyes too, because Jamie gave a sharp intake of breath, her own eyes going heavy-lidded.

Then she sighed. "This was a bad idea."

He swallowed. "We're adults, Jamie. We're perfectly capable of reining in this attraction and keeping things on a friends-only basis."

"Are we?"

Their gazes locked. Another burst of heat flared in his groin.

"We are," he said in a firm voice, though his tone didn't seem to convince either one of them.

Sighing again, Jamie reached for the small suitcase sitting on the seat between them. They'd stopped by the B&B to get her things, and the suitcase only served as a reminder that she would be staying with him. Sleeping in the room next to his. Possibly soaking in his Jacuzzi.

Cole gulped, then took the bag from her hands and hopped out of the truck. He rounded the vehicle to open her door and the two of them headed for the porch. After he unlocked the door and disabled the alarm, he dropped her suitcase on the parquet floor and glanced at her, suddenly noticing the disheveled state of her clothing. Dirt streaked her T-shirt and there was a small hole in her jeans, revealing the pale skin of her knee. His heart thudded again as he pictured her jumping out of a moving car.

"I should get cleaned up," Jamie said, noticing the sweep of his gaze. "Should I use the guest room you gave me the night of the storm?"

"Sure, and don't forget to take one of the painkillers the doc prescribed you."

She rolled her eyes, then brushed past him and climbed the wide staircase. "I don't need painkillers," she called over her shoulder. "I'm honestly fine, Cole."

He gave up on the pills—he knew a stubborn woman when he saw one. "Whatever you say, Agent Crawford. How about I make us some dinner?"

"Sounds good." Her voice was muffled; she was already disappearing into the second-floor landing.

Cole waited until she was out of earshot, then released a breath.

He wanted her, damn it.

And it drove him crazy, this insane need to claim her. The way they'd almost fallen into bed without a single concern for reason or consequence had reminded him far too much of his courtship with Teresa. He refused to jump into anything rash ever again, yet when it came to Jamie Crawford, he couldn't seem to remember the new set of rules he'd outlined for himself.

What was it about her that drew him in like a moth to a flame? Her intelligence? Her intriguing beauty? And what exactly did he feel for her? Gratitude, especially now that she'd gotten the truth out of Joe Gideon. Admiration, for the professional way she handled herself. Awe, that she could jump out of a moving car without hesitation.

And desire.

He glanced down at the erection straining against his jeans. Oh yeah, definitely desire.

With another heavy breath he rerouted his troubling thoughts, deciding to distract himself with dinner. An hour and a half later, as he removed a hot pan from the stove and set it on the cooling rack on the counter, he realized Jamie still hadn't come downstairs.

He wiped his hands on a dishrag, then trudged up the stairs and knocked on Jamie's door. When she didn't answer he went ahead and opened it, hoping he didn't catch her in a state of undress. Or maybe praying he *would*. But when he walked in he was surprised to find her sprawled on the burgundy bedspread, sound asleep.

His heart squeezed in his chest. She looked young and sweet while she slept, and not so obstinately professional. For all her easygoing smiles and casual tilts of the head, he'd noticed she was always alert, always observing and analyzing.

Trying not to wake her, he edged backward, only to jump when Jamie shot up in a blur, those shrewd lavender eyes fixed on him. "What's up?" she asked immediately.

He was impressed. "You're a light sleeper."

"Part of the job—always be prepared for anything." She rubbed her eyes. "Is everything okay?"

"I was just coming up to tell you dinner was ready, but if you want to keep napping, then—"

She was already off the bed and on her feet. "No, I'll come down. Just give me a minute to freshen up."

When she entered the kitchen ten minutes later, she was wearing black leggings, a red, hooded sweatshirt and her auburn hair was tied up in a high ponytail. He fought a smile.

In that getup, she looked more like a college coed than an FBI agent.

Her eyes widened when she spotted the food on the table. "Should I be insulted that you think my appetite warrants all this?"

"I wasn't sure what you liked, so I made a bunch of stuff."

He felt uncomfortable as she studied the feast he'd prepared. He'd planned on broiling a couple of steaks and serving them with baked potatoes, but at the last moment he'd realized he didn't know if she liked red meat, so he'd promptly boiled up some fettuccine, whipped up a rosé sauce and shoved some garlic bread in the oven. Then he'd questioned *that* choice and tossed a salad, grilling up some chicken to make it a hearty Caesar.

And now he felt like a total idiot.

"I guess I got carried away," he mumbled.

"Maybe just a little."

Her barely restrained laughter eased his nerves. He liked seeing her smile. There was something quite genuine about the way her mouth curved upward, the way her eyes twinkled with amusement.

They sat at the table and devoured the meal in silence. It wasn't until after he cleared the table and shoved several uneaten dishes into the fridge that Jamie spoke to him. As usual, she caught him by surprise.

"Do you have a lot of friends?"

He turned to face her, wrinkling his brow. "Why do you ask?"

She shrugged. "I don't know. I was just thinking about how angry Finn was with me, and it made me realize that if I didn't have Finn as a friend, I'd be all alone. I mean, I have my mom, of course, but the two of us are just so different it's kind of hard to consider her a friend."

Something shifted in his chest. "As much as that man rubs

me the wrong way, it's obvious Finn cares about you," Cole said grudgingly. "He's just worried. That's why he's angry."

"I know." She sighed. "I just wish he had more faith in me. I'm a trained federal agent. I can take care of myself."

Cole returned the sigh. "It's me he doesn't have faith in. He doesn't trust *me,* Jamie."

"I know, but it still irks."

As she sipped the red wine he'd poured for her, Cole thought about the question she'd posed at him, and discomfort crept up his spine. "No one," he found himself blurting.

She set down her glass and arched one delicate eyebrow. "What?"

"I don't have any friends," he clarified, his chest tight from the admission. "Sure, there are the people who want to be my friend, but not because they truly like me or want to get to know me. They're more interested in my wealth, or saying that they're close with *the* Cole Donovan."

"That must be tough, never knowing what someone's true motives are each time they say hello."

Still uncomfortable, he returned to the table and sat down, searching her face. "What about you? Why aren't you surrounded with friends?"

"My job," she confessed, circling her fingers around the stem of her wine glass. "I spent so much time building my career that I forgot there's more to life than work. And now I'm thirty-two, single, alone, and sometimes I feel like it's too late."

Her candid words fascinated him. "For what?"

"Children," she burst out. A twinge of embarrassment entered her voice. "A husband, kids, not an empty apartment and nothing to be proud of other than my badge."

"I know what you mean," he said quietly. "I want those things too."

Her skeptical laughter made his skin bristle. "I can't imagine you as a dad," she confessed.

Cole's irritation rose. "Why is that?"

"Because…well, because you're a multimillionaire. You travel the country and close nine-figure deals."

"So?"

"So…well…" She fidgeted. "I don't know…I just can't picture you as a family man."

Her words rattled him. Teresa had pretty much said the same thing to him when he'd raised the subject of having kids. Then again, Teresa hadn't *wanted* children. She'd much preferred spending all of his money and telling everyone she was married to Cole Donovan.

"Maybe I want to be a family man," he said, his tone harsher than he intended. "Maybe I want to be a husband and a father and stay in one place."

She had the decency to look shamefaced. "I'm sorry. I…I just assumed…"

"That I'm a coldhearted businessman who's only looking to close that next big deal?"

Her cheeks turned pink. "I…"

"I've had an offer to sell Donovan Enterprises."

His abrupt revelation made her eyes widen. "You did?"

"Ian told me about the offer when he dropped off the contracts the other day. At first I thought it was ridiculous, but now…" He shrugged. "Now I'm considering it."

Confusion etched into her features. "You're willing to throw away everything you've worked so hard for?"

"I threw it away before, when I gave away my father's legacy."

"But this is *your* legacy, Cole. *You* built this company."

"And Teresa's murder is destroying it." His throat clogged. "I don't know what I'll do. Selling is just something I'm thinking about."

"You can't let this investigation destroy everything you built," Jamie said in a gentle tone. "Gideon told the truth, and I'm sure when Finn takes the evidence to the district attorney, the D.A. will decide not to bring the case to the grand jury. It's too circumstantial."

"I've already been indicted in the press," he said darkly. "I didn't kill Teresa, but everyone will always wonder if maybe I did, if somehow I used all the money at my disposal to buy my freedom." A curse slipped from his lips. "And now the investigation is destroying *you,* Jamie. Someone tried to kill you, most likely the person who killed Teresa."

"Maybe."

Cole frowned at her. "What do you mean, maybe? Who else would want to hurt you?"

"I've put a lot of bad people away," she replied with a small shrug. "I wouldn't be surprised to learn that one of them has held a grudge."

"And one of these grudge-holders orchestrated your accident from behind bars?" Cole wasn't convinced. "That seems far-fetched."

"Just as far-fetched as your ex-wife's killer coming after me," she pointed out. "There hasn't been a single new lead since I came here. We're in no way closer to finding out who killed Teresa, and the killer has to know that. Why risk getting caught by tampering with my car? If I were the killer, I'd stay out of sight, keep my head down and out of trouble, and hope the investigation blows over."

"But you're not the killer, and you don't know what makes this guy tick or how he thinks."

She offered a tired smile. "Actually, I kind of do. I'm a profiler."

Cole blinked in surprise. This was the first he'd heard of it. "You're a profiler?" he echoed. "You don't go out in the field and investigate?"

"Not so much anymore. I started out as an investigator for the violent crimes unit, but now I work in the field office and go over crime reports to come up with usable profiles."

His wariness heightened. "So you try to get into the heads of killers?"

"Pretty much. I have master's degrees in Behavioral Sciences and Abnormal Psychology. I spend most of my time trying to figure out the personalities of violent offenders."

Cole wished she didn't sound so proud of the work she described. To him it sounded horrific, thinking like a killer, trying to understand what made violent people the way they were. For some reason, that bothered him far more than the thought of Jamie out in the field chasing after suspects.

"That's why I'm not certain the killer is responsible for my brakes failing," she added. "This man is too controlled, too precise. If he wanted me out of the way, he would have done it in a fashion that guaranteed it, not left it up to chance."

"Chance? Your car crashed into a tree," he grumbled.

"But I survived. When you kill by remote control, you can't guarantee your intended target will actually die. He would have been more active if he wanted me dead. A shot to the head, probably."

The grisly image she painted made his throat go tight. The more he got to know Jamie Crawford, the more he liked her, and the thought of her getting hurt—or killed—turned his veins to ice. She was here because of him. Because the woman he'd foolishly married had been murdered. And she was in this house because he'd promised to protect her.

Panic ignited his gut. What if he couldn't keep her safe?

"Uh…I'm going to go upstairs and take a shower," he said, his change of topic so abrupt it startled even him.

"Oh." Jamie blinked. "Okay. I should probably do that too. I fell asleep before I could wash all the dirt off me."

Their chairs scraped against the floor as they each got

to their feet. For one crazy moment Cole was going to suggest they shower together, but he bit his lip hard to keep the suggestion at bay. No. He couldn't sleep with her, damn it. He was in no shape for a relationship, and as he and Jamie walked upstairs in silence and headed for their respective bedrooms, Cole forced himself to remember that.

When Jamie stepped out of the shower a half an hour later and walked into the guest room, she heard the sounds of Cole moving around in the bedroom next door.

Maybe I want to be a family man.

As his words floated into her head, she sat on the edge of the bed, her towel riding up her thighs. A tiny burst of guilt filled her body. She knew she'd hurt him when she'd so carelessly assumed that their goals weren't aligned, but had she really been wrong to make the assumption? Men like Cole didn't settle down. They ran multimillion-dollar empires and worried about making money, not babies.

But, she did have to admit, Cole didn't seem at all concerned with money. And she couldn't believe he was actually considering selling his company. He wasn't at all what she'd thought he would be. He was definitely a shrewd businessman, judging by his success, and he emanated a deep sense of power, a self-assuredness that kind of turned her on. But he was more than that. Quiet in an intense sort of way, intelligent, funny when he let down his guard. And he could cook better than the chef at her favorite restaurant in Charlotte.

Why would a woman ever throw away a man like that?

Teresa had done it, and now Jamie was doing the same thing, fighting her growing feelings for the man because... because of what, really?

Murder investigation.

A sigh flew out of her mouth. It always came back to this damn case. But why should it? She'd been with the Bureau for ten years, and not once had she gotten involved with some-one connected to a case. Or someone who *wasn't* connected. Truth was, she'd only had one serious relationship, if you could count six months as *serious*.

Why couldn't she put aside her professional obligations just this once, and be with Cole? It didn't even have to lead to a relationship. She liked him, he turned her on and she truly believed he wasn't a criminal. Would it be so wrong, having a brief, albeit passionate, fling with the man?

Quit overanalyzing everything to death and go next door already.

A hysterical laugh tickled her throat. Yep, story of her life, wasn't it? Overanalyzing. She did it every day at the office, and the annoying trait that worked wonders when it came to picking apart a crime was most certainly a hindrance to her personal life.

Tired of acting like a Negative Nancy, Jamie lifted her chin in resolve and strode out of the room. She experienced a pang of apprehension as she stood outside Cole's door, but she shoved away the doubt and gave a soft knock.

He opened the door bare-chested, momentarily turning her brain into a pile of mush. She stared at the sculpted muscles of his chest, the defined pecs and washboard stomach, then shook herself back to reality and met his dark eyes. "Can I come in?"

His heated gaze took in the white terry cloth wrapped around her body. "I don't think that's a good idea," he said in a raspy voice.

"Maybe not, but I'd still like to come in."

After a moment of discernible hesitation, Cole moved aside so she could enter, but she noticed he kept several feet of distance between them. "What's going on?" he asked.

Her hand toyed with the top of her towel, where she'd

tucked it so it would stay up. Cole's eyes instantly began to smolder as he followed the movements of her hand.

"I know we shouldn't do this," she murmured. "I don't have sex with men I've only known for a few days. Actually, I hardly ever have sex." Her cheeks scorched. "I can't even remember the last time I did."

"Jamie—"

"No, let me finish." She swallowed to bring moisture to her arid mouth. "I don't have time for relationships. I spent my entire life working my ass off so I could get out of that trailer park and make something of myself. And now here I am, about to throw it all away because you're so darn attractive."

His lips twitched in amusement.

"It's not funny," she said with a sigh. "I *know* this is a bad idea, Cole."

It was hard to breathe with the waves of awareness bouncing between them, hard to move with her legs wobbling like JELL-O, but she managed to bridge the distance between them. Inhaling deeply, she placed her hand on his bare chest. Her pulse took off when she felt the wild hammering of his heartbeat beneath her palm.

Cole's throat worked as he gulped. "Nothing will come out of this, Jamie. Even if we give in, I'm in no place for a relationship."

"I'm not sure I am either," she admitted. Her fingers tingled as she stroked the hot flesh of his chest. "But I don't think I can fight this any longer. I…I *ache* for you."

Arousal flashed in his eyes, strengthening her confidence. Fine, so this was crazy. Her job, the ongoing murder investigation, Cole's issues about his ex—the obstacles in their path were hard to ignore.

But tonight, she wanted to pretend there was nothing in their way.

Just for tonight.

Gathering up some more confidence, Jamie dropped her hand from Cole's chest and moved it to the top of her towel. Then she took a breath and let the towel fall to the floor.

Chapter 11

Cole felt as if he were in a trance as he stared at Jamie's beautiful naked body. Every inch of her was total perfection. Her high, full breasts tipped by dusky red nipples. Her small waist and long, silky legs. His mouth went bone dry, then flooded with moisture as she reached up to undo her ponytail, causing her breasts to jut out enticingly. She let her hair loose and the auburn waves cascaded down her slender shoulders.

Get out. Protect your heart.

The swift warning made his gut clench, but for the life of him, he couldn't fight the desire sizzling through his body. Still, he made a last-ditch effort to stop this runaway train before it picked up speed. "We shouldn't do this," he murmured. "You need to walk out that door, sweetheart."

Her gaze heated from the endearment, and he realized that this was the first time he'd called anyone that. With Teresa, it had been *babe*. Never anything as tender as *sweetheart*.

"Or I can stay," she murmured back, stepping closer.

At the feel of her nipples tickling the hair on his chest, Cole smothered a groan. Every muscle in his body was coiled tight, his restraint in desperate danger of crumbling. He needed to touch her. Just one touch, and then he'd stop this madness.

Taking a deep breath, he lifted his hand and stroked one golden shoulder. "Your skin feels like silk," he rasped.

Your skin feels like silk? He wanted to kick himself for using such a cheesy cliché on her, but it was the truth. Jamie's smooth flesh slid underneath his palm, hot and satiny, making his pulse drum in his ears.

Lord, he couldn't stop this. With her warm, naked body pressed against his, his control was obliterated. He wanted Jamie Crawford. Had wanted her from the moment he'd laid eyes on her.

She must have seen it in his eyes, because she gave a faint smile and said, "Yes?"

"Yes," he choked out.

Her hand came up to his chest, eliciting a low groan from his lips. "I need to touch you," she whispered. "I need to… God, I don't know what I need."

Although it was pure torture, he stood motionless and let her explore, clenching his teeth as her delicate fingers traveled over him. She stroked the center of his chest, then moved toward one flat nipple and touched it with the tip of her finger.

Cole hissed out a breath.

Jamie froze and gave him a questioning look.

"Don't stop," he muttered, close to passing out from sheer pleasure. "Keep touching."

She did. Teased his other nipple, then tickled the hair on his chest, following the narrow line down to his waistband. When she slipped her fingers underneath the elastic of his boxers, he gave an involuntary thrust of his hips. Her hand met his waiting erection. Her lavender eyes widened.

"Cole," she murmured.

He moistened his dry lips. "Yeah?"

"I don't know what's happening to me." She gazed up at him, her face a mixture of passion and confusion. "I'm not usually like this. But with you... I *want* you. I want..."

She didn't finish. He wouldn't have let her anyway, the need to kiss her so strong he had no choice but to give in. Their mouths found each other. The kiss sucked the breath from his lungs and he nearly keeled over. With a low growl, he yanked her onto the bed and covered her body with his. They kissed again, hot, openmouthed kisses, tongues dueling and chests heaving.

"I want to taste every inch of you," he muttered against her moist lips.

"Later," she muttered back, her hand finding his arousal again. "Right now I just want you inside me."

She didn't need to ask twice. Somehow he scrambled off the bed and found a box of condoms in the bathroom. He was sheathed and ready by the time he lowered his body over hers again, flames of anticipation licking at his skin. When he slid into her, they both groaned, hoarse, strangled sounds that hung in the heated air.

"Oh, my God," Jamie choked out, lifting her hips to bring him deeper. "So good...it's so good..."

All he could do was mumble something incoherent in return. *So good* was an understatement. His entire body was coiled tight. The feel of Jamie's warmth surrounding him was too much. *Too* good. Knowing he was in danger of losing complete control, he forced himself to go slow, to draw out Jamie's pleasure before he exploded into oblivion.

"More," she begged, winding her arms around his shoulders and digging her fingernails into his skin.

He stared down at the beautiful woman beneath him, at the tousled dark red hair and swollen, thoroughly kissed lips and that last thread of restraint snapped like a bungee cord. With a groan, he let go, thrusting into her over and over again, until the haze clouded his vision again and every inch of his body ached with impending release. When he heard her cry out, felt her tighten against him in climax, he threw that last ounce of control into the wind.

As pleasure exploded around him, he knew without a doubt that his entire world had just been changed.

When Jamie crashed back to earth a few minutes later, the lingering ripples of pleasure were replaced with a wave of panic. Panic so strong her throat tightened and her palms began to tingle.

From the corner of her eye she saw Cole's impressive chest heaving as he regained his breath, the hard ridge of his arousal, the sated expression on his face. Her body reacted instantly, a fresh dose of desire shivering through her veins which just intensified the frantic pounding of her heart.

Unable to stand it, she bounded out of the bed as if she'd just discovered a cockroach between the sheets.

"Jamie?"

Cole's deep voice, tinged with caution, only succeeded in heightening her panic. Avoiding his eyes, she edged toward a doorway to the left, hoping it was a bathroom as she said, "I'm just going to get cleaned up."

She hurried into the bathroom and closed the door behind her, then drew in a calming breath and moved toward the sink, where she splashed cold water on her flushed face.

Her reflection in the large mirror showed a woman who'd just been thoroughly satisfied, and she had to move her eyes away. Unfortunately her gaze landed on the black marble

Jacuzzi Cole had told her about earlier, which just turned her on again as she pictured making love to Cole in that tub.

"Snap out of it. It was just sex," she muttered to herself. "Chill out, Crawford."

Her fretful brain clung to the reassurance. Just sex.

Fine, *great* sex.

All right, the best sex of her life.

She promptly bent down, cupped some more water between her palms and doused her face again. When she'd come to his room, she'd been fully prepared to sleep with him. She just hadn't thought it would be so…explosive. Was that how sex always was? How it was supposed to be?

A soft knock rapped on the door. "Jamie?"

Shutting off the faucet, she took another long breath, then straightened her shoulders and opened the door. She found Cole standing there, as naked as she still was, and there was a knowing look in his eyes.

"You panicked," he said frankly.

As her cheeks went hot, she crossed her arms over her chest to shield her bare breasts. "A little," she admitted. "I… that was really good, Cole. *Too* good."

"Is there such a thing?"

His gruff voice and the crooked smile he shot her chipped away at the alarm that had had been coating her throat.

She gave a rueful shake of the head. "I'm being silly, aren't I?"

"No, just cautious," he said softly. "And if I'm being honest, what happened between us just now got me a little scared too."

"Really?"

He stepped toward her, gloriously nude and looking oddly vulnerable. "I've never had sex like that before. Intense…out of control…"

He trailed off, and the slight bewilderment in his husky

voice banished the last of the worry from her body. Was there really any point in second-guessing herself now? She'd already given in to temptation and fallen into bed with the man. And sure, a relationship probably wasn't in the cards, but that didn't mean they couldn't continue to explore this attraction for a bit longer.

Exhaling, she slowly uncrossed her arms and let them drop to her sides. Cole's black eyes instantly dropped to her chest, leaving splotches of heat on her skin. Her nipples tightened painfully, and moisture gathered between her legs. Cole didn't make a move toward her. He seemed content with simply looking, and after several long seconds, she groaned in frustration.

"Kiss me," she ordered.

His mouth quirked. "Are you sure?"

Jamie sighed. "We might as well finish what we started."

"I thought we already finished," he said with the teasing tilt of his head.

"Then let's start again."

Before she could blink, he'd scooped her up in his powerful arms and was laying her down on the bed, his big body covering hers. Their mouths found each other, latching together in a kiss that left her hot and breathless.

She ran her fingers over his sinewy back, breathing in his familiar scent of spice, musk and soap. When his hand moved between her legs, she moaned, parting her thighs so he could tease her into oblivion. Pleasure gathered in her belly, dancing along her bare skin.

"Cole," she choked out, reaching between them in search of his erection.

Her intentions were clear, but he ignored the unspoken plea. Instead, he slid down her body and placed his mouth on her aching core, officially stealing all coherent thought from her brain.

She fisted the silk sheets as he made love to her with his lips, his mouth, his tongue. The sensations were almost unbearable. As her muscles went taut and her moans grew more anxious, Cole promptly climbed back up, and then he was sliding inside her in one long, delicious thrust.

Jamie came apart, her entire world exploding as stars flashed in front of her closed eyelids. She clung to him, digging her fingers into his firm buttocks as he moved inside of her in a fast, crazy rhythm.

When her heartbeat regulated and the last ripples of release faded, she found him staring down at her with heavy-lidded eyes, his sexy mouth tilted in a pleased smile. She suddenly realized that he hadn't climaxed, that he was still hard and throbbing inside her.

"You didn't..." She groaned as he started to move again, igniting another spark of passion in her sated body.

"Nope," he confirmed, answering the unfinished question. His hips rolled, eliciting a sigh from her lips.

"Last time was too fast," he added, his voice rough, his eyes glittering with arousal. "This time..." He pulled out, then thrust in again.

"This time what?" she squeezed out, dying from his sensual ministrations.

"This time I'm going to take it nice and slow, sweetheart." His mouth brushed over hers in a fleeting kiss. "All night long."

"I'm too tired to move," Cole mumbled the next morning, burrowing his head under the covers. "Just call me when the coffee's ready."

Jamie burst out laughing. She was already dressed in a pair of blue cotton shorts and an old Duke University T-shirt, and for some reason, she was wide awake and feeling energized, despite the endless rounds of mind-blowing sex they'd indulged in last night. Apparently their time between the sheets achieved the opposite effect on Cole, who had so far resisted every effort she'd made to drag him out of bed.

"Come on," she cajoled. "It's a beautiful morning. Sun is shining, birds chirping. You're missing out."

"Stop being so damn chipper," came his muffled voice. "I deserve some much needed rest after what you put my body through."

She laughed again, but decided to give up. "Fine, I'll go downstairs and make a pot of coffee. I'll give you a shout when it's ready."

"Thank the Lord." He proceeded to roll onto his side and pull the covers over his head, effectively dismissing her.

Rolling her eyes, Jamie left the bedroom and headed down to the kitchen where she clicked on the coffee machine, then drifted to the patio door. It really was gorgeous out, the sky a cloudless blue and the sun high in the sky, its light reflecting off the sliding glass door. After pouring herself a cup of coffee, she reached for her purse, which she'd left on the kitchen counter, and rummaged around for her cell phone. With a steaming mug in one hand and her phone in the other, she stepped out on the cedar deck overlooking Cole's backyard.

She inhaled the warm morning air, then sipped her coffee and admired the yard. It was enormous, large enough to house a swimming pool, but evidently Cole hadn't wanted one. Not much of a swimmer?

Her chest went tight for a moment as she realized she really didn't know much about the man whose bed she'd shared last night. He ran a real estate empire, built things with his own two hands, but what else? What did he do for fun? What books did he enjoy reading?

That she didn't have the answers to those questions troubled her. What exactly was she doing here? And why did it bother her so much that she didn't know every last detail about Cole? When she'd decided to act on her attraction, she'd told herself it would only be a fling, that for once in her life, she wanted to act on impulse instead of worrying about the consequences. But sleeping with him was one thing. Wanting to *know* him was an entirely different matter.

Setting her coffee on the wooden railing, she flipped open her phone and punched in Finn's number, needing a distraction from her muddled thoughts. But when Finn answered, he sounded just as angry as he'd been yesterday at the clinic.

"Still alive, I see," he said in lieu of a greeting.

Her jaw tensed. "Come on, Finn, there's no need to be a jerk. I told you why I went with Cole."

"Right—for his security system."

She ignored the sarcasm dripping from his voice. "Would it kill you to admit that Cole is innocent?"

"And ignore the evidence against him?" He hurried on before she could protest. "Circumstantial, I know. But guess what, circumstantial evidence can still send a man to jail."

Frustration curled around her spine, making her antsy. Descending the wide steps of the deck, she stepped barefoot onto the grass and began to pace, a habit that always reared its head when she was feeling particularly annoyed. "Joe Gideon saw Cole in the woods at the time Teresa was murdered. Cole didn't kill her."

"Then who the hell did?"

Her pacing intensified. "I don't know," she said in irritation. "It's hard to come up with a profile when there's absolutely nothing to go on. I told you already, our guy is—"

"Neat, analytical, reserved," Finn cut in. "Yeah, I remember. But how exactly does that help us? We still have to *find* the bastard. Unless we already have, and you're just refusing to admit it."

"Cole didn't do this," she said through gritted teeth. "He couldn't have."

Why, because you're sleeping with him?

She banished the mocking voice right out of her head, refusing to believe there was any truth to its taunt. She may have slept with Cole, but sex hadn't completely wiped away her common sense. Or her professional instincts. Her gut was telling her that Cole had nothing to do with his ex-wife's death. They just needed another suspect. Another clue. Anything that could help her make sense of this murder that seemed determined to remain unsolved.

She quit pacing, suddenly noticing just how far she'd walked from the house. Somehow she'd ended up a hundred yards away, near a cluster of trees with thick branches that swayed in the morning breeze.

"There has to be something we're missing," she said as she headed back in the direction of the house, the grass tickling her bare feet. "We just need to—"

A sharp crack suddenly exploded through the air and pain streaked through her shoulder!

With a cry, she stumbled forward. The phone fell out of her hand, landing on the grass, and she could hear Finn's tinny voice yelling, "Jamie? *Jamie?*"

She touched her right shoulder, shocked when she lifted her hand and saw it was stained crimson.

Dear God, she'd been *shot*.

Chapter 12

Cole had been trudging down the stairs, rubbing the sleep from his eyes when he heard a loud boom. His spine instantly stiffened, adrenaline filling his veins as he realized the noise had sounded suspiciously like a gunshot.

A *gunshot?*

As his pulse raced off in a wild gallop, he sprinted to the kitchen. "Jamie?"

But the room was empty, and when he noticed the open sliding door he streaked through it, bursting onto the deck in time to see Jamie tumbling to the grass fifty yards away. She clutched her shoulder as she went down, and Cole fought a jolt of sheer panic.

The adrenaline spiked, propelling him into action. Without a solitary thought about his own well-being, he dashed toward Jamie, half expecting another shot to ring out and hit him in the chest.

He skidded to a stop in front of her, sinking onto his knees and launching himself at her. He got her flat on her back, shielding her with his own body as he moved his head from side to side to make sure nobody burst out of the trees. Moisture seeped into his shirt and his heart jumped in alarm when he looked down and noticed the blood pouring out of Jamie's shoulder.

She'd been shot. Someone had *shot* her, on his goddamn property!

"Are you okay?" he demanded.

She nodded, looking dazed. "I'm fine. It was just a graze."

"Just a graze?" he echoed in disbelief. "You were shot, Jamie! By a *bullet!*"

"Yeah, that's usually what comes out of a gun."

Her cavalier reply had him seeing stars. Maybe getting hit by a bullet was no major event to her, but to him, it was a freaking *big deal!*

He lifted his head again, scouting the area, but the woods at the edge of the yard were quiet, save for the soft rustling of the trees and the happy singing of the birds. The shooter must have positioned himself somewhere in the trees. The motion sensors only surrounded the house and the perimeter of the yard, but not beyond that, which meant that someone had been in the woods, watching the house.

Although Cole was loath to get up and risk the gunman taking another shot at them, Jamie was bleeding like a stuck pig beneath him. Maybe she was right and it was just a graze, but there was too much blood for his liking.

"Come on, we've got to get you inside," he told her. "Keep your head down, okay?"

To his relief, she did as he asked, hunching over once they stood up. She had her hand clamped on her wound as they ran in the direction of the house. The sight of the sticky red blood marring her skin brought a rush of fury to his gut. The person responsible was going to pay for this. Cole would make certain of it.

"How's the arm?" he asked urgently.

"It stings. But I've had worse."

Fighting the urge to lift her into his arms and carry her the rest of the way, Cole squeezed her hand tighter, not once relaxing his grip until they were in the safety of his kitchen.

"Sit down," he barked. "I'll get the first-aid kit." He paused in the doorway. "On second thought, I'll drive you to the clinic."

"No way," she grumbled. "Just get the damned kit."

When he returned to the kitchen a minute later, Jamie had taken off her T-shirt. She wore only a snug black sports bra and she'd slid down the right strap so it didn't constrict her shoulder.

A lump of terror lodged in Cole's throat. Blood was caked on her golden skin. He had to wonder if the shooter had aimed for the arm, or simply missed Jamie's head, or heart or whatever the intended target had been. Either way, Cole swallowed down the terror, along with a dose of relief that she was alive.

She didn't make a single sound as he cleaned up the wound, not even when he dumped a generous amount of iodine on her skin to sterilize the laceration. He knew it must have stung like hell, but Jamie didn't even twitch.

After he'd cleaned it, Cole examined her shoulder, realizing she was right. The bullet had only grazed her skin, leaving a nasty-looking burn and taking off some skin. He quickly bandaged up the area, then walked over to the sink to wash his hands.

"Cole" came her hesitant voice.

He turned around slowly. "Don't say it's no big deal."

"I wasn't going to. I was just going to suggest we call Finn.

Though he's probably on his way over. I was on the phone with him when the shot rang out."

"I'm already on it," Cole said as he reached for the cordless phone on the counter.

"Good." She finally winced, revealing the first flash of pain and discomfort he'd seen since she was shot. "And maybe you can grab those painkillers from upstairs. I think I might actually need them this time."

He knew admitting any weakness was probably a strain for her, so he decided to bite back the urge to order her to lie down or something. She didn't seem to have any intention of getting off the chair and he decided to give her that. As he headed upstairs to get the pain pills, he dialed Finnegan's number, and when he reentered the kitchen a minute later, Jamie was where he'd left her, the elbow of her good arm propped up on the table. "Did you call Finn?"

"Yeah. You were right. He was already on his way," Cole reported as he got her a glass of water.

He handed her the water and two painkillers, which she swallowed without any objection. It was only after she drained the glass and leaned back in the chair that Cole finally let himself relax. The adrenaline racing through his blood slowly dissipated, leaving him numb and unbelievably angry with himself. He'd been supposed to keep her safe, keep her protected. Someone had cut her brakes the day before, for chrissake. He should have locked her in the damn house. Refused to let her out of his sight.

He stared at her in dismay. She looked small and fragile sitting there in nothing but a sports bra and those little blue shorts, with her red hair coming out of her ponytail. A smudge of dirt marred her silky cheek, and there were grass stains on her knees. He wanted to take her into his arms and never let her go, which was almost as disturbing as the fact that she'd just been shot on his property.

How had Jamie gotten under his skin in such a short amount of time? When he'd given in to the attraction last night, it was only supposed to be about sex.

"Why do you look so serious?"

Her gentle voice penetrated his thoughts and he met her eyes. "You could have been killed," he said, clenching his fists to his sides. "Christ, it's like every woman I get involved with is destined to lose her life."

A strange look flitted across her face. "Cole—"

"Maybe I should get you out of town," he interrupted. "I've got a place in Tahiti that we can—"

"No way. I'm not leaving Serenade."

"Even if it means you getting killed?"

She stuck out her chin. "I'm going to be here to catch this guy. I don't run and hide when things get a little dangerous."

"A *little* dangerous?" The rest of his irritated speech went unfinished as the keypad by the door buzzed, indicating someone was at the gate. Apparently Finnegan hadn't wasted any time in getting here.

After pressing the button to open the gate, Cole glanced at Jamie's sports bra and frowned. "You should put something on."

"Why?" She suddenly laughed. "Because of Finn?"

"Yes, because of Finn," he snapped back.

"Trust me, he doesn't look at me that way."

Cole doubted it. The bra she wore covered everything, but did nothing to hide the fullness of Jamie's breasts, or the flat expanse of her creamy stomach. Still, she made no move to reach for her bloodstained shirt.

"If he even looks at you funny," Cole threatened.

She must have heard the contempt in his voice because she laughed again. "What are you going to do, beat him up?"

He glared at her, ready with a comeback, but then the doorbell rang and he strode off to let the sheriff in. When Finn burst into the kitchen and spotted the white bandage covering Jamie's upper arm, he let out a curse that had Cole raising his eyebrows.

"Did you see the shooter?" Finn asked immediately.

"No," Jamie answered. "But he was definitely behind me. Probably hiding in the woods somewhere."

"Where were you, exactly? I need the precise location." After Jamie relayed the information, Finn dialed a number on his phone and spoke to his deputies, who were apparently on their way.

He hung up, saying, "Max and Anna will comb the woods. They've got the forensic tech with them, so if there's any trace evidence, he'll find it."

As Jamie had predicted, Finn didn't even seem to notice her scantily-clad appearance. After a cursory glance at her bandage, he gave her a deep scowl. "Now I'm getting you out of here. No arguments, Jamie."

Cole wasn't surprised when she argued. "I'm not leaving."

Finn just gaped. "This house is evidently not as safe as you insisted. You were just *shot,* damn it. Where was the damn security system?"

"The motion sensors only go off when someone reaches the edge of the yard," Cole spoke up. "The shooter was obviously beyond the perimeter, somewhere in the woods."

Finn turned to glare daggers at him, but spun around when Jamie held up a hand and said, "I thought of something."

The sheriff's expression displayed an irritated flicker. "What, that you should get the hell away from this man?"

"No," she said, looking just as annoyed. "I had an idea about why Teresa might have been killed."

Finn faltered. Cole could sense the other man still wanted to argue some more—it was probably what he did for fun— but Jamie's revelation was too tempting for either man to ignore.

"Pour me a cup of coffee, Donovan," Finn barked. Then he glanced at Jamie. "I'm listening..."

Cole bristled at the sheriff's coffee demand, but at least the other man seemed willing to quit scowling at everyone and actually listen to Jamie. So, swallowing his pride, Cole moved to the counter and prepared coffee for a man he didn't particularly like, pouring himself a cup too.

They gathered at the table a few moments later, and Jamie spoke with the pensive slant of her head. "Cole said something before you got here," she told the sheriff, "about how it feels like the women in his life are targets."

Finn's face turned red, as the implication behind Jamie's words settled in. Cole expected the man to explode at the thought of a romantic connection between Jamie and his main suspect, but Jamie hurried on, quickly diffusing the bomb before it went off. "It got me thinking about why. *Why* is someone coming after me? Since I got here, we haven't come up with any new leads about who the killer might be.

"The killer has no reason to want me off the case," she continued. "Especially considering we've got zilch for leads. Maybe if we were getting close, sure. But I can't see this guy making a preemptive strike *just in case* I happened to figure it out. He's too smart to stick his neck out like this, to risk getting blamed for trying to kill me. He got away with killing Teresa—I'd imagine he'd want to stay out of sight and hope he remains in the clear. Which makes me think we've got the motive all wrong."

Cole was extremely intrigued. And quite fascinated by the way her brain worked. "What do you mean?"

"We've been assuming that Teresa was killed because she pissed someone off, because someone wanted to hurt *her*." Jamie's voice went grave. "But what if that person was trying to hurt *you*?"

"Me?" he said in surprise.

"Think about it. You're a powerful businessman, I'm sure you've made some enemies over the years. Maybe the reason we can't catch the man who killed your ex-wife is because he's not *connected* to your ex-wife. Maybe he's connected to you."

Finn let out a reluctant-sounding breath. "You might be onto something, Crawford. Maybe someone's trying to get at Donovan here."

The object of the discussion shook his head. "That's ridiculous. Teresa and I were divorced. Anyone who read the tabloids knew that killing her wouldn't cause me much pain."

"It would if you're then implicated in her murder," Jamie pointed out. "Your company's already suffering because of it. Maybe that was what the killer intended."

"Come on, Donovan," Finn mocked. "I'm sure you stepped on some toes on your way to the top. You must have pissed a few people off."

Cole wrinkled his forehead in thought. "No," he said, confidence ringing in his voice. "I built my company honestly, with integrity. I didn't want to do it the wrong way, the way my…"

He didn't finish the sentence, but he knew Jamie had filled in the blanks. *The way my father did.* But talking about his dad in front of the sheriff was about as appealing as painting his toenails pink, and he had no desire to give Finnegan more ammunition against him. Poor Cole Donovan and his crappy relationship with his daddy. Finn would pounce on that like a hungry lion.

"I have some professional enemies, sure," Cole admitted. "Some guys I may have outbid on certain projects." He paused. "George Winston comes to mind, but I can't see the man going on a murder spree to get back at me for outbidding him. Competition is the name of the game. Anyone who gets into real estate development knows that."

"What about disgruntled employees?" Jamie asked. "Someone you might have fired, someone who left the company with a bad taste in their mouth?"

Helplessness jammed in his chest, causing him to shrug. "I don't think so, but I can look into it. I've got a very discreet P.I. I use from time to time. I was actually considering calling him to run his own side investigation about Teresa's murder, but—" he shot Finn a stony look "—I figured you wouldn't appreciate the interference."

"How generous of you," Finn said, sarcasm dripping from his voice.

Cole ignored the barb. "But I'll give him a call now, see what he comes up with."

"It's worth a shot," Jamie said. "Sure, we can keep digging around and try to sift through the endless amount of people who hated Teresa, but someone has tried to kill me twice. And since my presence on the case is hardly threatening, what with *all* the progress I've made, it makes more sense that I'm a target because someone is after you, Cole."

Because they were involved. She didn't say it, but the telltale blush on her cheeks said everything. Finn noticed it too, and frowned.

Cole ignored a nudge of annoyance. So what if the sheriff didn't approve? He and Jamie were both consenting adults. They didn't owe Finnegan any explanations.

"It's an angle we can't ignore," Finn admitted in a grudging tone. "If our guy is going after the women in your life, then it's most likely someone you know."

"I'll call my P.I.," Cole said again.

With a nod, Finn pushed away his mug and stood up. "Come on, Jamie, let's go."

She remained in her seat. "I already told you, I'm staying here."

Finn looked livid. "So someone can shoot you again?"

"I won't leave the house this time. I pretty much painted a target on myself by walking out in the yard. I was distracted and didn't think."

"You're still not thinking," Finn grumbled. "Just because this theory of yours makes sense doesn't mean he—" he jerked a hostile thumb at Cole "—isn't a threat to you."

Jamie let out a sigh. "I'm perfectly safe with Cole."

Though her conviction brought a rush of warmth to his chest, Cole suddenly had to question the truth of her statement. *Was* she safe? It sure hadn't felt like it an hour ago.

But could he really let her leave? Every protective instinct he possessed told him not to let this woman out of his sight. Great sex aside, he genuinely liked her, and the memory of watching her fall to the grass with a bullet wound to her arm tore at his insides.

Maybe they didn't have a future, maybe great sex was all they'd ever have, but Cole suddenly realized that until Teresa's killer was caught, he was not going to leave Jamie Crawford's side.

"I hate it when he's angry with me," Jamie confessed as she and Cole settled in the living room after Finn was gone.

Her friend had made several more attempts at getting her to leave with him, but Jamie had stood her ground and Finn had eventually left in a huff. She hadn't liked the angry way he'd stormed out, but it wasn't enough to change her mind. Cole wasn't to blame for what happened earlier. She'd gotten shot because *she'd* been foolish, because she'd been so frustrated with the lack of progress on the case that she'd stupidly drifted to the other end of the yard without thinking that anyone might be out there.

But who had shot her? Why was someone watching Cole's house? It troubled her, and apparently it bugged Finn too, because he'd arranged to have his deputy Max stand guard in the woods for the next couple of days. Jamie had a feeling the mysterious shooter would be long gone though. He had to know that the forest wouldn't be safe for him to hide out in any longer.

"He's worried about you," Cole said. "Frankly, so am I."

She curled up on one end of the couch, resting her head against the plump arm. She was feeling a tad sluggish thanks to the painkillers she'd taken. It was probably the sluggishness that didn't make her object when Cole scooted in beside her and wrapped his arms around her from behind. The position was too romantic, too intimate, but at the moment, the feel of his strong embrace was incredibly soothing.

"This is nice," she murmured.

"It is," he murmured back.

"By the way, what did your private investigator say when you called him?"

"He's fully on board. He's going to start investigating all my employees and business contacts. Discreetly, of course."

"Good."

"I also spoke to Ian," Cole told her, gently skimming his fingers up and down her uninjured arm. "Apparently the company that wants to buy me out doubled the offer."

"Really?"

"Yeah."

He went quiet, and they lay there in comfortable silence. Jamie couldn't remember the last time she'd felt this content. Surprising, since only an hour ago she'd been flat on the grass dodging bullets. But the serenity also succeeded in making her edgy. This thing with Cole was about sex, not intimacy. Even if she wasn't investigating his ex-wife's murder, they probably still couldn't make it work. She lived in Charlotte, was pretty much married to her job. He lived in Chicago when he wasn't in Serenade, with a job that was just as demanding. He was a millionaire, she came from a trailer park.

As uneasiness moved through her body, Jamie twisted around to meet his dark eyes. "What are we doing here?"

"Well, we're lying down on the couch, and in a bit, you should probably take a nap because, after all, you were *shot*."

"You know that's not what I meant."

He swallowed. "I know."

"Are we being foolish? I mean, I know we have chemistry together, but neither of us want a relationship. So why bother? Why spend all this time together when it won't go anywhere?"

His chest heaved as he exhaled. "I don't know." He hesitated, then spoke in a gruff voice. "All I know is that I like being with you."

She bit the inside of her cheek. "I like being with you too. I feel so comfortable with you, Cole. And I like how you don't seem bothered by my job. A lot of men think a woman doesn't belong in law enforcement."

"Well, I can't say I like that you hang out with killers all day long, but I respect what you do, Jamie."

It warmed her heart to hear him say it. In the past, her career had gotten in the way of her relationships, a cold snippet of reality that had made her wonder if she'd ever find a man who could respect her work.

"I respect what you do too," she told him. "Even if you do end up selling your company."

"I don't know what I want to do," he confessed. "Ever since I moved to this town, I've had a tough time leaving. I'm not sure I want to travel so much anymore."

She totally understood. Everything was so simple and beautiful in Serenade.

Except for the crazed killer roaming about.

The memory caused her to sigh. "There's no reason to

even talk about this. Neither of us is in a position to make any kind of real decisions until we find whoever killed Teresa."

"And whoever's trying to kill you," he said roughly. His arms tightened around her. "I won't let this bastard hurt you again, Jamie. I swear, I'm not letting you out of my sight until we catch him."

Her heart did a somersault, and suddenly her vocal chords had a life of their own. "I don't know what I feel for you," she whispered. "Mostly confused."

"Tell me about it. I've been confused since the day you showed up at my door."

She shifted around again and saw the bewildered expression on his chiseled face. "I truly didn't think I'd ever want to be in another relationship," he added. "After the divorce, I shut down."

"That's understandable. People tend to do that after they've been badly hurt."

"I was more than hurt," he said hoarsely. "That woman destroyed me. I gave her everything I had and she always demanded more. In the end, I had nothing left."

"You have a lot left," she said, bending close to brush her lips over his.

His tongue teased the seam of her lips, bringing a shiver to her skin. He kissed her softly, one hand toying with her hair, which she'd released from her ponytail. He played with the auburn strands as his mouth moved over hers. After a few breathless moments, he pulled back and said, "You should really take that nap. You just got shot."

"I'll do it only if you join me."

"If I join you, we won't get any sleep," he growled.

His reply made her grin, and the confusion and indecision she'd felt a moment ago dissolved as she leaned in to kiss him again. Who needed to talk about the future? For the first time in her life, she was living in the moment, focusing on something other than her job, and right now, she wanted to cling to that liberating feeling just a little bit longer.

"I don't need sleep," she murmured. "Maybe if the bullet went through…but it was just a graze, and the cure for grazes isn't sleep."

He shot her a dubious look. "Yeah, then what's the cure?"

"Sex. Lots and lots of sex."

Chapter 13

Cole smiled as he stared at the sleeping woman in his bed, memorizing every beautiful detail before quietly leaving the bedroom and closing the door. He headed downstairs and made some coffee, then sat at the table and wondered what the hell he was doing.

He and Jamie had spent the entire afternoon in bed, only coming up for air so he could draw them a luxurious bubble bath in the Jacuzzi. Afterward, he'd ordered her to lie down on the bed and proceeded to pamper her with a full body massage that had them both groaning with pleasure and impatience. His clothes had disappeared soon after and he'd tugged her onto his lap and let her take the lead this time, worried that he might hurt her shoulder if he was on top. Jamie had straddled him, moving in a slow, sexy rhythm that drove him wild, and when they both exploded with passion, she'd rolled over, closed her eyes and promptly fallen asleep.

And now he was alone, sifting through a pile of con-

flicting emotions and asking himself how on earth Jamie
Crawford had managed to break through the shield he'd con-
structed around his heart. He shouldn't want her this much.
He shouldn't care this much.

He was done with relationships, unwilling to take another
risk and let down his guard. Truth was, Teresa's betrayal had
done a number on his pride. She'd cheated on him. Lied to
him. Made his life a living hell. And yeah, Jamie was nothing like Teresa. She was kind, compassionate, patient, but
that didn't mean she didn't have the power to destroy him.

And he refused to let another woman have that much
power over him.

Cole closed his eyes, wondering how and why his life had
turned into such a mess. It wasn't just his growing feelings
for Jamie weighing on his mind. It was also the business.
He couldn't quite explain it, but ever since Ian had told him
about Lewis's offer to buy the company, he hadn't been able
to stop thinking about it. A year ago the idea of selling his
empire would have sent him into gales of incredulous laughter. He was thirty-four years old, one of the richest men in
the country, and if he wanted to, he could stay at the top for
a very long time. Retirement had always seemed eons away.

But everything changed once Teresa died. He'd been
forced to stay in Serenade, ordered not to leave town, and
in the time he'd been here, he'd felt...at peace. For the most
part anyway. Yes, he had this murder investigation lurking
in the shadows of his life, but he wasn't restless, or even all
that motivated to return to Chicago and go back to work full
time. Aside from answering emails, doing teleconferences
and looking over the blueprints and contracts Ian brought,
he wasn't too involved with the running of the company anymore.

And he kind of liked it.

What had come over him? He loved his work. Loved staring at empty lots and envisioning the structures he could put up there. How had he become bored and unhappy with the job without even realizing it?

The ringing of his cell phone ended his troubling reverie. A glance at the caller ID showed Hank Shaw's number, Cole's private investigator.

"That was fast," Cole said in lieu of hello. "Got something already?"

Hank chuckled on the other end. "Yes and no. Just wanted to tell you I did a quick check on George Winston. You said you wanted me to look into him first, right?"

"Yeah. What'd you find?"

"Nothing much. Aside from having the reputation of being an ass, Winston is squeaky clean. I did a soft check on his finances and nothing suspicious stood out to me, not in the company account, or his personal checking account."

Cole didn't bother inquiring how Shaw had managed to look into Winston's personal and company bank accounts. There were some things you simply didn't ask your P.I.

"I also managed to get into his date book and home calendar—"

Again, Cole didn't even ask.

"—and he's got an alibi for the night your ex-wife was killed. And he's alibi'd for the past three days too. He was in Boston with his wife. Airline confirms it."

"Could he have hired someone to kill Teresa and go after Jamie?"

"Maybe, but again, there was nothing fishy about the finances. No large withdrawals that indicate he may have paid someone to do his dirty work."

Cole frowned, but he wasn't really surprised. It had been incredibly far-fetched, the thought that a business rival was involved in Teresa's death. There might be bad blood between them, but Winston didn't strike him as a killer.

"Thanks for the update, Hank. Anything else I should know?"

"Word around town is that Winston is gloating over your current predicament," Hank said in an apologetic voice. "He's spoken to several bankers and urged them to cut your financing."

"Shocking," Cole mumbled to himself. Out loud, he said, "Thanks again, Hank. You're looking into Donovan Enterprises next?"

"Yep, I got the email you sent."

The email in which Cole had pretty much given the investigator a key to the company. Pass codes that would allow Hank to access employee computers through a back door, passwords for personnel files, staff evaluations, everything only Cole was privy to. He hated giving Shaw such free rein, but with Jamie's life potentially at stake, he wasn't taking any chances.

"I'll be in touch," Hank said. "Expect an initial report on past employees in twenty-four hours."

Cole thanked the man for the third time, then hung up the phone and sighed. A part of him still couldn't accept Jamie's suggestion that the killer might be after *him*. He'd always prided himself on his integrity, the honest way he did business. To think that someone might despise him and was plotting to hurt him was a concept he couldn't reconcile.

"Uh-oh, why do you look so serious?"

Jamie's quiet voice came from the doorway. His head lifted as she entered the kitchen, wearing nothing save for one of his long-sleeved shirts. The material hung down to her knees, the same cute knees that had straddled him just an hour ago.

"I talked to the investigator," he said as she walked over and sat in his lap.

The feel of her firm, warm bottom against his groin made

him shudder with pleasure. Lord, he would never tire of this woman. Everything about her turned him on beyond belief.

Trying to quell the desire rising in his body, he continued the recap of his conversation. "He checked out one of my competitors and didn't find anything suspicious. Doesn't look like the guy is involved in any of this. He's looking into my employees now."

Jamie rested her chin on his shoulder. "If he doesn't come up with anything, we could always look at Valerie Matthews."

"Valerie? Where did that come from?"

"I don't know. I just have a bad feeling about her. It seems like she's always getting in my face, and that's a red flag for me—people who get too involved in ongoing investigations."

He nodded. "Yeah, she is pretty vocal about this case. But I'm pretty sure Valerie has an alibi for that night. She was out of town at some office retreat."

"And now she's first in line yelling at everyone to send you to jail. You know, law enforcement would be so much easier if the murderers just did their thing and then came in to confess."

He threw his head back and laughed. "Ever the optimist."

With a giggle, Jamie hopped out of his lap. "A girl can dream." She headed for the fridge. "Is there anything to eat? Because I'm starv—"

There was a loud buzz, causing Cole to groan in irritation. "Now what?" he muttered as he stumbled to his feet and headed for the intercom. He pressed a button and barked, "Yeah?"

"Donovan, it's Finn," a voice crackled. "I need to speak to you."

Again? Cole was tempted to tell the sheriff to get lost, but then realized this might be about Jamie's shooting. Had Finn found something already? Quickly opening the gate, Cole left Jamie in the kitchen and went to answer the door, hoping

the sheriff was here to deliver the good news that the shooter
had been apprehended. When he opened the door, however,
he was taken aback by the grave look on Finn's face. Oh no,
this definitely wasn't a good news visit.

Finn stood on the porch, his shoulders tense, his expression clearly saying *I don't want to be here right now.*

Cole glanced past the other man's broad shoulders and
spotted a second vehicle in the driveway, occupied by Deputies Holt and Patton. A police cruiser and Finn's Jeep. This
couldn't be good.

"Finnegan…what's going on?" Cole asked warily.

The sheriff briefly closed his eyes, then opened them to
reveal a flicker of pleading reluctance. "Please don't give me
trouble here, all right? I'm just doing my job."

"Finnegan…"

"I need you to come with me."

Cole's stomach went rigid. "Pardon me?"

"Christ, I don't enjoy having to do this, okay?" Finn exhaled a ragged breath. "But I need to bring you into the station for questioning."

Jamie heard Cole's outraged voice from the porch and
promptly shut the refrigerator door. She hurried to the front
entrance, her bare feet slapping against the hardwood. She
didn't know what she was expecting to find, but it wasn't the
sight of Cole and Finn facing off with their faces inches apart
as Cole said, "I'm not going anywhere."

"What the hell is going on?" she demanded.

Finn gave her pained look. "I need Cole to come into the
station. And willingly, because I'm not in the mood to use
my handcuffs on him."

"What? *Why?*"

Finn ignored her and turned back to Cole. "Come on, Donovan, don't do this."

Jamie stepped between the two men, glaring at Finn. At five-nine, she was a tall woman, and nearly at eye level with her friend. "Finn, tell me what's going on."

Finn glanced at Cole, then at Jamie. With a sigh, he edged backward and gestured for her to follow him. "Give us a second, Donovan."

Jamie battled confusion as Finn led her over to his Jeep, where he crossed his arms over his broad chest and lowered his voice. "We found the gun, Jamie. The murder weapon."

"What? When did this happen?"

"About an hour ago. The operator at the town dump found a forty-five caliber Smith & Wesson by a pile of construction debris."

"So?"

"So the bullet the coroner fished out of Teresa came from a forty-five. The ballistics guy just tested the gun and determined it was the one that fired that bullet."

Jamie frowned. "What does this have to do with Cole?"

"Anna got the logs from the dump—there's a record of everyone who goes there, the trash is weighed, recorded, the whole deal." Finn gave a reluctant pause. "Cole was there, Jamie. Three days after Teresa died."

Shock slammed into her. "Finn...so what if he went to the dump? That doesn't mean he tossed the gun."

"Maybe not, but I still need to bring him in."

Anxiety swam in her belly. "Cole didn't kill his ex-wife. You have to believe that."

"I don't know what to believe anymore. But do you honestly expect me to ignore this? You're a federal agent, damn it. You know I need to bring him in for questioning. You would do the same thing in my place."

As much as she hated to admit it, he was right. Forcing herself to forget her personal involvement with Cole, she thought about what she would do in Finn's position, if she'd discovered that Cole could be linked to the place where the murder weapon had been found.

What would *she* do?

"Okay. Okay." She sighed. "You're right. Just let me talk to him for a moment."

"Convince him to come in without a fight, Jamie. I don't want a scene here, not in front of my guys."

Drawing in an unsteady breath, she walked back to the porch where Cole stood with a stoic expression. "Cole," she started. "You need to—"

"No," he cut in. "Don't tell me to cooperate. I didn't do anything wrong, and I'm not going anywhere with that man."

"You have to," she said sadly.

His eyes flashed with anger.

"He'll arrest if you don't. So please," she pleaded, "go to the station. I'm sure this will all be cleared up in no time."

"*What* will get cleared up?" Frustration thickened his voice. "What the hell is happening?"

"Go to the station, Cole. Finn will explain everything."

"Why don't *you* explain it to me?"

"Because I can't. I can't get involved in this." She was frustrated too now, and she could feel Finn's unhappy gaze burning a hole in her back. "Please, do what he says. I'll get dressed and meet you there, okay?"

After a second of obvious reluctance, Cole gave a bleak nod. "Fine. But only because you asked, Jamie."

Relieved, she glanced at Finn and nodded imperceptibly.

He took that as his cue to advance, and when he reached them, she met his tense blue eyes and said, "Can you ask your deputies to stay while I put some clothes on? I'd like to meet you at the station. I'd drive Cole's pickup but the painkillers are still in my system."

Finn's face softened. "No problem." He quickly instructed

Anna and Max to stick around, then turned to Cole. "You ready, Donovan?"

"What the hell do you think?" Cole muttered, but he didn't put up another fight as he followed Finn down the porch steps.

Jamie had never felt so helpless as she watched Cole get into the passenger seat of Finn's Jeep. She waited until they drove off, then flew into the house and bounded upstairs. She threw on one of her sleek black suits, left the jacket unbuttoned, and hurried back downstairs to slip into a pair of comfortable black flats.

Neither Anna nor Max spoke to her during the drive to the station, but she noticed the sympathy in Anna's brown eyes and knew the younger woman felt bad about this new development. Jamie still couldn't wrap her head around it. Cole might have visited the place where the murder weapon had been stashed, but that didn't make him a killer. Lots of other people had probably been to that dump. Someone else must have planted the gun at the dump, and Cole's visit was just a coincidence. There was no other explanation.

"We're here."

Anna's soft voice drew Jamie from her thoughts. She was surprised to see that they'd reached the station. Without waiting for the deputies, she jumped out of the backseat and raced into the building through the rear door. She figured Finn would be in one of the interrogation rooms with Cole, but instead she found him in the hallway, rubbing his forehead and looking utterly frazzled.

"Is everything all right?" she demanded.

Finn looked ready to tear his hair out. "No, everything is not all right. He lawyered up."

"What?"

"I told him why I brought him in, how we found the gun,

and he said some very unladylike words and demanded a lawyer."

Jamie closed her eyes. Oh God. A morning shooting and an afternoon arrest. This day just kept getting worse and worse.

"Please tell me you let him make the call," she said with a sigh.

"Of course I did. I'm aware of the whole 'you have a right to an attorney' part of the Miranda. Only thing is, his lawyer's flying in from Chicago, so the guy won't be here for another two hours."

A headache began to form at her temples. She reached up to massage the ache, wondering how everything had spiraled out of control in the blink of an eye.

"What about my shooting?" she finally asked.

Finn blinked. "What about it?"

"Did your deputies find anything in the woods, a shell casing? Maybe my shooter used the forty-five and then went to the dump and got rid of it? Because if that's the case, it couldn't have been Cole. He was in the house when I got shot."

"We didn't find any evidence in the woods," Finn replied, promptly bursting her bubble. "And the dump operator said nobody dropped anything off today, which means the gun was already there when you got shot."

Disappointment crushed her chest. "Okay. Fine. What about prints then?"

"Our forensics guy is testing it now."

"Cole didn't do this," Jamie whispered. "He couldn't have done this."

"Why? Because you're sleeping with him?"

She stared at him in disbelief. "I can't believe you just said that."

"I'm sorry, but it needed to be said." He lowered his voice.

"You can't just ignore evidence because you're obviously sweet on the guy. He was at the dump. The gun was at the dump. He wanted his greedy ex-wife out of the picture. She died. What do you expect me to do? Look the other way?"

Jamie was surprised to feel tears stinging her eyelids. Oh God. Not now. She didn't cry. Ever. And this wasn't the time to start.

"I know you care about him," Finn finished, his tone so infinitely gentle her tears threatened to spill over. "But you're a professional, honey. And we're splat in the middle of a murder case."

"I know." She cleared her throat, trying to control her emotions. "You did everything by the book, Finn. I'm sorry if I made you feel otherwise."

Their eyes locked for a moment, and the empathy on his face was almost too much to bear. She knew he was right. As an investigator, she couldn't disregard evidence just because it pointed to a person she cared about. She had to think logically here, remain neutral and open-minded and forget that the man in that interrogation room happened to be the one who'd made incredible love to her only hours ago.

She took a breath. "Let me talk to him."

"I don't think that's a good idea, Jamie."

"We both know he's not going to talk to you. So unless you want to wait two hours for the lawyer to show up, you need to let me speak to him."

Chapter 14

Cole lifted his head when Jamie walked into the room, relief pounding inside of him like tribal drums. Thank God. Maybe now they could put an end to this ludicrous mess. When the sheriff had told him that the murder weapon had been found—at the place where Cole had dropped off some damn garbage a couple of weeks ago—he'd wanted to laugh out loud. Instead, he'd cursed like a sailor in a fistfight, unable to believe that this was actually happening.

Teresa was making him as miserable in her death as she had in life. When would it all end, already?

"Hey," Jamie said, her voice quiet. "Are you okay?"

He gestured around the barren room, from the narrow table to the plain white walls. "What do you think?"

She looked at him with tired eyes, then sat down on the chair in front of him. Not next to him, he noted with growing unease.

"Let's talk about why you went to the dump three days after Teresa died."

His jaw tensed. "Are you kidding me?"

"Cole…please." Her expression became tortured. "Just talk to me. This isn't an official interview. I just want to make sense of this."

Despite the warning bells going off in his head, he forced himself to see her point of view. The discovery of the murder weapon was a shock to everyone. Maybe if he convinced Jamie that this whole thing was a stupid coincidence, she'd talk to Finnegan on his behalf.

"I went there to dump something," he muttered. "Isn't that why people go to a dump?"

"What did you get rid of?"

Indignation coursed through his blood. The implication was crystal clear and he didn't appreciate it one bit. "Jesus, Jamie, do you actually think that if I killed my ex-wife, I'd leave the damn murder weapon where anyone could find it?"

"Then what did you drop off?"

"Garbage," he said through clenched teeth. "Branches, construction stuff. I had just finished building the shed and there was a lot of wood and sawdust and other crap. Would you like me to describe every piece of trash? I think there were some banana peels, paper towels, tea bags—"

"Cole." She sighed.

The agony in her lavender eyes did nothing to ease the anger bubbling inside of him. It only got worse with her next question.

"Have you ever owned a gun?"

His jaw dropped. "I can't believe you're asking me these questions."

"Have you?"

"No, I have never owned a gun." Disdain dripped from every word. "I also didn't kill my ex-wife."

"Did you ever come into contact with a Smith & Wesson forty-five? Maybe a friend owns one and you held it once, admired it?"

"No." The fury boiling in his gut spilled over, toxic waves of it pumping in his bloodstream. "Who exactly am I speaking to here?" he demanded.

She looked startled. "What?"

"Am I talking to Jamie, the woman I made love to this afternoon, or *Special Agent Jamie Crawford?*"

"Both," she said, sounding anguished. "I don't like doing this, but I understand why Finn had to bring you in."

"Unbelievable," he muttered.

Her voice grew desperate. "You told me you respect what I do, that my being in law enforcement doesn't bother you. And I promised Finn to assist him on this case. Why can't you see that I have a job to do?"

"Bull," he shot out, his hands trembling with anger. He laid them flat on the table, resisting the urge to start overturning chairs. "You're not even here officially, and once we slept together, you shouldn't have been on the case at all."

"Maybe not," she whispered.

Their gazes locked. Cole battled a fresh rush of indignation. "You know I didn't do this, Jamie."

"The gun—"

"Screw the gun! You know in your gut that I didn't kill anyone." Every muscle in his body coiled tight. "I thought we meant something to each other."

"We did. We *do,*" she corrected. "But you said so yourself, we don't even have a future."

"We might have," he said quietly. "But now that you're choosing your damn job over me, I can't see how that will ever happen. Christ, why are you ignoring your common sense and questioning me about something I didn't do?"

A sheen of tears glistened in her eyes, but her obvious distress did nothing to calm him down. She didn't trust him, he realized. Maybe enough to have sex with him, but not enough to believe in him. Hell, it didn't matter what she believed anymore. Her job was evidently more important. His reputation, his pain, it meant nothing to her.

The insecurity niggling at him didn't help him keep his cool. What was wrong with his judgment lately? He hadn't seen Teresa's true nature until it was too late, and yet again he'd misjudged the female in his life. He'd thought Jamie was sincere in her assurance that she was open-minded, but clearly she wasn't. Clearly, the *evidence* meant more to her than his word.

"I'm done talking," he muttered. "I think I'll wait for my lawyer."

"Cole, I'm not doing this to hurt you," she blurted out, tears clinging to her eyelashes. "I'm just trying to make sense of all this, about the gun, why it was found where you—"

"I did not leave that gun in the dump," he snapped.

"I'm just—"

"Doing your job. Right, I got that, loud and clear." He crossed his arms over his chest in a tight shield. "And I'm going to wait for my lawyer."

"Cole—"

"I mean it, *Agent Crawford.* I'm not saying another damned word until my attorney arrives."

Jamie paced the hallway outside the interrogation room, alternating between anger and self-loathing. She still couldn't believe that Cole had banished her from the room like that. That he refused to see that she was simply trying to get to the bottom of this mess.

His words of accusation had been branded into her brain, and as she waited for the interview to end, she had to wonder if she'd handled this all wrong. She truly didn't think Cole had killed his ex-wife, but in the face of this new evidence, what else could she have done? Any other suspect would have been brought in to the station for questioning. Any other suspect would have needed to answer the questions she'd put in front of Cole.

Then again, she wasn't in love with any other suspect.

She stopped in her tracks.

She was in love with Cole?

How could she be in love with him? She'd only known him for such a short time.

She sagged against the wall, unable to control the pounding of her heart. Light-headed, she blinked back tears and drew in several long breaths.

Right now, Cole was inside that room with his lawyer, forced to answer Finn's questions, and instead of being by his side, she was out in the hall like the bad cop asked to leave the premises.

Her stomach clenched. Her promise to Finn had overruled her relationship with Cole. Maybe Cole was right and she should have recused herself from the case.

Her mind continued to race, a carousel of emotions spinning around until she could barely function. When footsteps sounded from the end of the corridor, she jerked her head up, frowning at the unfamiliar man advancing toward the door of the interrogation room. He wore a pair of thick black glasses and had a brown file folder tucked under his arm. Acknowledging her with a nod, he knocked on the door and waited.

When Finn stepped out into the hall, the new arrival handed him the file, then shot a dubious glance at Jamie.

"You can speak freely, Tom," Finn said. "Jamie's with the FBI."

"Oh. All right." The man shoved his glasses up the bridge of his nose. "The gun is clean. Not even a partial print."

Finn didn't look surprised. "That's what I figured. Anything else?"

"The serial number was filed off, so it will be impossible to trace, but I took some digital pictures of it. You can have your deputy send them to Raleigh, maybe the folks there can gauge where it might have come from, but I warn you, there aren't any distinguishable marks on the piece."

Finn's knuckles tightened over the edge of the folder. "Wonderful. Then we've got no leg to stand on." He shot Jamie a grave look. "We can't hold him."

She nodded numbly. She wasn't surprised by the forensic tech's findings either.

"It could still be him," Tom the tech offered, evidently mistaking her reaction for disappointment. "He probably just wiped the gun before dumping it."

Jamie's lips tightened, but she didn't object. Sure, maybe Cole *had* wiped the gun. If he was the killer.

But every fiber of her being told her that Cole was innocent.

Yet she'd interrogated him like a common criminal...

You did your job!

She clung to that, the reminder that she was a professional first and always had been. She might have fallen for Cole— God, hadn't that realization come out of left field?—but she was still a federal agent, and if he cared about her like he claimed, then he needed to understand that her job was important to her. It *defined* her.

"I'll be in the lab if you need me," Tom spoke up. He shook the sheriff's hand, gave Jamie a timid smile, then walked off.

"I can't keep this from them," Finn said, holding up the folder.

"I'll wait here," she murmured.

Finn disappeared into the interrogation room, and less than two minutes later the door flew open again with a loud thud. A man in his forties stepped out first, boasting a head of silver hair, hawklike features and a scowl. Cole came out next and Jamie's heart ached at the sight of his lifeless expression.

"Cole," she blurted out.

He didn't even spare her a look. "Come on, Martin, let's head over to the house so we can discuss this."

Jamie's face collapsed. As client and attorney whisked off, she stared at Cole's back, the proud set of his shoulders, the dark hair gleaming under the fluorescent lights in the hall. She wanted to go after him but her feet were rooted in place.

"That was unnecessarily harsh," Finn remarked, disapproval ringing in his tone.

Jamie couldn't even voice her agreement. Her throat was too tight, a vise of anger clamped around it. How could Cole blow her off like that, as if she were nothing more than a casual acquaintance he'd run into on the street?

"Well, what are you waiting for?" Finn asked. "Go after the jerk."

Snapping out of her turbulent thoughts, she curled her hands into fists and hurried after Cole. She caught up to him and his attorney just as they were reaching the front lobby, and when she called out Cole's name his entire body went as rigid as a board. He muttered something to his lawyer and the other man nodded and exited the police station.

Looking as if he'd rather be just about anywhere else, Cole strode toward her with a frown. "What is it, Jamie?"

Her nostrils flared. "Really? That's how you're going to handle this? By leaving?"

"There's nothing to handle. You made it clear where you stood back in that interrogation room."

"Enlighten me then. Where do I stand, Cole?"

"You're more concerned about your job than you are about us," he said flatly.

"That's not true," she protested. "I told you why I had to ask those questions. It wasn't personal, damn it."

"Wasn't personal?" he echoed in disbelief. "Everything about this is personal! You've been staying at my house, sharing my bed—how is that *not* personal?"

"And I'm helping the sheriff solve a case," she replied in a calm voice. "You can't expect me to ignore that just because we're sleeping together."

"That's what it comes down to then." He shoved his hands into the pockets of his jeans. "You can't ignore your job because it's the only thing you care about, Jamie. It's your entire life."

"And yours isn't?" she shot back. "You worked hard to build your company. Well, I worked hard too. I dragged myself out of a trailer park, waitressed my way through junior college, busted my butt to get the grades I needed to transfer to Duke. I didn't sleep for four years! I slaved to get to this place in my career and I'm not going to apologize for loving what I do, or for wanting to keep on doing it."

He didn't seem to hear a word she'd said. "Your career will always come first for you. You just proved that."

She went silent. It suddenly dawned on her what this was about. God, how could she have been so blind?

"We never stood a chance, did we?" she said sadly.

He looked stricken. "That's not true."

"Yeah, it is. Know why? Because you're not over Teresa."

Her quiet accusation hung in the air, the silence broken by Cole's harsh laugh. "I got over that woman long ago."

"But you're not over what she did to you." Sorrow lodged in her throat. "She betrayed you. She wounded your pride."

"Are you trying to profile me?" he muttered.

"No, just calling it like I see it." She shook her head. "We should have never started this up. You said so yourself, you weren't ready for a relationship, and I see now that you were right. You haven't worked through your issues about your ex-wife."

"Don't turn this around," he said in a low voice.

"I think you were just waiting for an excuse to push me away," she murmured. "You didn't want to admit that making another commitment actually terrifies you, so you pretended you were fine with getting involved with me, all the while waiting for a reason to back out."

He frowned at her. "You interrogated me as if I was just another criminal."

"I went in to get your side of the story," she corrected. "Because I'm in love with you."

He gave a sharp intake of breath.

"But my feelings don't matter," she said, ignoring the painful constriction of her chest. "This was a mistake. This entire…thing between us. You're not over Teresa's betrayal and the fact that your own judgment failed you. And instead of dealing with it, you've decided to accuse *me* of a betrayal I didn't commit. Maybe I shouldn't have gone into that room, but I did it because I wanted to help you. Those questions would have been asked regardless, I thought it would be easier if they came from me."

Her hands shook as she reached up to rub away the tears forming at the corners of her eyes. She wasn't even sure she'd gotten through to him. His rugged face revealed nothing, not a single iota of emotion.

With a sigh, she took a step back. "Take care of yourself, Cole."

When he didn't respond, she simply cast a last sad look in his direction, turned on her heel, and walked away.

"They don't have a case," Martin Worthington declared as Cole walked the older man to the door.

Martin had said the same thing in the kitchen as the two

men discussed the case over coffee, and Cole felt better thanks to his attorney's confidence. Better about the investigation, anyway. About the heart-wrenching confrontation with Jamie…well, he was still ravaged from that.

"Just do as the sheriff requested and stay put," Martin continued, tucking his black leather briefcase under his other arm so he could shake Cole's hand. "And don't worry. The gun isn't registered to you, your fingerprints aren't on it, and even if the DNA results put your skin cells under Teresa's fingernails, you have an alternative explanation. She grabbed you in front of witnesses. Trust me, Cole, this won't even go to trial."

"Thanks, Martin." He gave the attorney's hand a firm shake, then bid him goodbye and closed the door.

The moment he was alone, an unsteady breath left his mouth.

Everything Jamie had said to him kept replaying through his head like reruns of a bad TV show. She'd been completely off base, accusing him of looking for a reason to push her away.

That was insane. Wasn't it?

During his conference with his lawyer, he hadn't let himself consider Jamie's words. As far as he was concerned, she'd gone from a lover to a stranger when she'd marched into the interrogation room and acted like an emotionless federal agent.

Now, in the solitude of his home, he allowed himself to think about what she'd said.

He walked to the kitchen door, his gaze drifting out at the backyard. It was surreal to think that she'd been shot this morning. So many crappy things had happened since then, and the sun was only now beginning to set.

As hues of pink and orange filled the sky, Cole finally opened his heart to permit the truth to slide in.

Jamie was right.

Damn it, she was right.

A part of him had always wondered how his judgment had failed him so completely when it came to his ex-wife. Teresa had revealed her true colors within months of their wedding. She'd let down the mask and the wife he'd adored had turned into a cruel, selfish monster who went out of her way to hurt him.

He'd spent many long nights thinking about how foolish he'd been, how blind. Teresa had sliced up his pride with a blade of spite and hatred. He'd vowed to never let another woman humiliate him like that again, and when Jamie had started asking all those questions…Christ, that same sting of humiliation returned, making him lash out.

He hadn't understood Teresa's true nature until it was too late and he still didn't know how he hadn't seen it. But he did know one thing, and that was that he'd totally blown it with Jamie back there.

The sound of vibrating snapped him back to reality, and he turned away from the door and fished his cell phone out of his pocket.

"Donovan," he said briskly. At the greeting of the unfamiliar voice, he furrowed his brows. "Who? Oh, Pierre…hey, what's up?"

He listened for several disturbing seconds, then said, "No, stay put. Let me call you back with instructions."

Hanging up, he quickly punched in another number from memory, letting out a relieved breath when his private investigator answered on the first ring. "Hank, it's Cole. I need you to drop what you're doing and check something for me."

Chapter 15

Well, you knew it couldn't last.

With a noisy exhale, Jamie shoved the pessimistic thought out of her mind and took a sip of the coffee she'd just poured without waiting for it to cool. Maybe if the liquid scalded her throat she might be able to ignore her aching heart. She'd been sitting in Finn's office for the past twenty minutes, lost in a private pity party.

She kept wondering if Cole was all right, if his lawyer was assuring him at this moment that there was no case against him, but then she realized it was none of her concern anymore. Cole didn't want anything to do with her, all because she'd done her job and questioned him in that interrogation room. To make matters worse, her shoulder was beginning to throb again, now that the effects of the painkillers she'd taken earlier were wearing off.

"Want me to drive you to the B&B?"

She looked up to see Finn in the doorway. "I checked out,

remember?" she said with a sigh. "And all of my stuff is at Cole's."

"I can pick it up for you, if you'd like. And you can come stay with me. I'll even call the alarm company and have my system updated."

She knew he was trying to help, but not even his gentle tone could ease the ache in her chest. "Sure, whatever you want," she murmured.

"Jamie, I know you're upset, but—"

He was interrupted by the hurried sound of footsteps, and then Max Patton, Finn's second deputy, rushed up to the door. "Boss, a 911 call just came in."

Finn's shoulders went stiff. "What have we got, Max?"

"A body," the younger man said, his features creased with tension. "The caller wouldn't give his name, but he said he stumbled over a body in the woods behind Joe Gideon's house."

Jamie sucked in her breath. "Joe Gideon?"

Max nodded. "I'm not sure if Gideon was the caller, or if it's his body the caller was referring to—the guy hung up before I could ask."

Finn was already removing his car keys from his pocket. The gold sheriff's badge clipped to the belt on his jeans glimmered as he turned for the door. Jamie got to her feet too, but Finn quickly gestured to the chair. "No, you stay here," he ordered. "You're still woozy from the painkillers, and I can't have you getting hurt."

She wanted to argue, but the brief rush of dizziness she experienced from standing abruptly told her that Finn was right. She was in no shape for a walk in the woods right now. "Call me when you know something?" she said instead, sinking back on the chair.

Finn nodded. "The second I know what we're dealing with."

Without another word, Finn and his deputy dashed out of the office, their footsteps thudding in the bullpen. A moment later they were gone, and Jamie sat in silence, reaching up to rub her suddenly throbbing temples. A body. Gideon?

Or what if...

Icy fear filled her veins. Gideon's property was right next to Cole's. What if something had happened to Cole?

Tamping down her panic, she drew in a calming breath and forced herself to stay put. She couldn't go running off on her own. She didn't have a vehicle, anyway. And Finn had said he'd call when he knew something. Which meant she had no choice but to sit in his office and wait for news.

Ten minutes passed, Finn still hadn't called and Jamie's worrying intensified. Whose body had they found, damn it?

Please, don't let it be Cole.

She shot to her feet, deciding the only way to ease her worry was to find out for sure. She would call Cole, just to make sure he was okay. He probably was. Hell, he was probably sulking at home, still angry with her.

She'd left her purse on one of the desks in the bullpen, and she made a beeline for it, finding her phone just as a familiar voice came from behind.

"Sitting around doing nothing," Valerie Matthews remarked coldly. "Why am I not surprised, Agent Crawford?"

Stifling a groan, Jamie turned to face the other woman. "Hello to you too, Valerie."

Teresa Donovan's sister directed a scowl in Jamie's direction. "You promised to keep me posted about the case."

"I did. I mean, I am," she corrected.

"Really, then why did I have to find out from Tom Hannigan that you have the gun that killed my sister?"

Ignoring the dull throb of her shoulder, Jamie crossed her arms over her chest. Tom Hannigan? The lab tech, she remembered. Then she frowned, annoyed that someone involved with the case would reveal crucial information to a civilian.

"We did find the gun," she conceded. "But it was wiped of fingerprints and the serial number was filed off. We have no way of knowing who it belongs to."

"Cole Donovan, obviously," Valerie muttered.

At the sound of Cole's name, Jamie glanced at the cell phone in her hands. Damn it, she *had* to know if he was all right. "Look, Valerie, I'm kind of busy at the moment. Maybe you can come in tomorrow and the sheriff and I will update you on—"

"Update me now," Valerie interrupted, her eyes flashing with anger.

"I can't. I was actually about to call Finn to tell him to pick me up," she lied. "He's supposed to drive me over to his house."

"Fine. I'll drive you."

Jamie narrowed her eyes. "No, thank you. I'll just wait for Finn."

"You need a ride. I need answers about my sister's *murder*," Valerie snapped. "And I'm going to get my answers, damn it. This has gone on long enough."

A tremor of suspicion climbed up Jamie's spine. Why was Valerie insisting? And why had she shown up here out of the blue?

Right after Finn received a 911 call that had him rushing out of the station.

Something didn't add up. She felt like she was looking at a missing piece of the puzzle, but couldn't seem to fit it in place. She looked into Valerie's dark gray eyes and the suspicion grew stronger. Did Valerie know something? About Teresa's death? About the attacks on her?

"Okay," Jamie finally agreed, an edge to her voice. "You can drive me to Finn's."

"Good, and you can answer my questions," the other woman retorted.

With reluctance weighing down on her chest, Jamie followed Valerie out to the parking lot, where a shiny white Honda Civic was parked. Valerie unlocked the doors and, with a mocking gesture, motioned for Jamie to get in. Still uneasy, Jamie slid into the sleek leather interior, then waited for Valerie to get in.

She had to find out what Valerie knew. If the woman even knew anything. Maybe the painkillers she'd taken were making her mind jumbled, steering her instincts on the wrong course. Either way, she intended to find out.

Valerie put the car in Drive and pulled away from the curb. "Why the hell haven't you arrested him yet?" the woman demanded. "You've got the murder weapon now."

"Have you ever stopped to think that maybe Cole didn't kill your sister?" Jamie asked in a quiet voice.

"Of course the son of a bitch killed her!" Valerie tossed her black hair over her shoulder in outrage. "And he's going to kill you too, if you keep hanging around him."

Jamie sighed. "Seems to me like the only person making threats about me dying is you, Valerie."

"Oh, trust me, honey, those were just warnings." Valerie gave a hard laugh. "I haven't even started with the threats yet."

Cole was stunned as he hung up the phone, unable to comprehend what his P.I. had just revealed. Hank had kept him on the line while he looked into Cole's request, and the entire time, Cole had clung to the hope that this was a mistake.

Now, it was glaringly apparent that that wasn't the case, even as his brain continued to fight the obvious. It was too appalling to even consider. She couldn't have done that. She *couldn't* have.

She did, an irritated voice buzzed in his head. *So deal with it and do something.*

Christ, he had to find Jamie. He was probably overreacting here, but if what Hank said was true, then there was a chance she was in trouble.

Big trouble.

Darting out of the kitchen, he paused only to swoop up his keys from the credenza in the front hall and put some shoes on. Fighting the panic rushing inside him, he stumbled down the porch steps towards his truck, determined to find Jamie and make sure his suspicions were unwarranted. Of course she was okay. There had to be a logical explanation for what Hank had discovered.

He reached the truck, then halted in his tracks.

Eyes widening, he stared at the tires in disbelief, wondering if he was imagining it. As his pulse pounded between his ears, he knelt down, then let out an obscenity.

All four tires had been slashed. And not just once. Someone had taken a knife to them and sliced so many holes in the thick rubber that driving would be impossible.

It must have happened when he was being questioned at the station, and he hadn't noticed the damage when Martin had dropped him home. He'd been too distracted at that point. Too devastated.

With a growl of frustration he tore back into the house and skidded into the kitchen, where he grabbed his phone from the counter and dialed Jamie's number. As the ringtone chimed endlessly in his ear, dread climbed up his spine.

"Damn it, Jamie, pick up."

"Hi, you've reached Jamie Crawford. I'm unavailable to take your—"

"Damn!"

Cole quickly controlled his rage before he gave in to the impulse to whip the phone across the room. With stiff fingers, he dialed a different number, and the sheriff's gravelly voice filled his ear. "I'm in the middle of something, Donovan. This had better be important."

"In the middle of what?" Cole demanded. "Is Jamie with you?"

"No, she's at the station. I left to answer an emergency call. False alarm, though."

Cole's spine stiffened. "What are you talking about?"

"Someone reported finding a body on Joe Gideon's property," Finn said, sounding impatient. "But there's nothing here. We just searched the area where the body was supposedly found, didn't see a damn thing. And Gideon is now getting in my face, threatening to sue me for harassment because we interrupted him in the middle of a damn bender. Now what the hell do you want, Donovan?"

Finn was at Gideon's, which meant he could get here in no time, Cole realized. "Look, I need you to come and pick me up. Someone slashed my tires, probably when I was at the station with you, and I have no way to—"

"Someone slashed your tires?"

"Yes. So get over here, Finnegan." He swallowed a lump of panic. "I think Jamie's in danger."

"What are you talking about? What's going on, Donovan?"

"I'll explain everything when you get here." Cole spoke quickly, urgently. "Just hurry."

A click sounded in his ear. He could only hope that Finn had hung up without a word to save time and was running to his car at this very second. Gideon's cabin was only a five-minute drive, the sheriff could make it here in less than that if he ignored the speed limit.

Cole bounded to the security room to unlock the gate, then went out to the porch, where he fixed his gaze on the end of the driveway, as if he could will Finn's Jeep to appear. It must have worked, because the Jeep burst onto the dirt path a minute later. Cole was in the passenger seat before the vehicle came to a complete stop and then Finn did a sharp turn and barreled down the driveway again.

"Where are we going?" he demanded.

"My house." Cole's lips tightened. "Where Teresa died."

"Are you going to tell me what the hell is going on?"

The trees on the side of the road whizzed past like streaks of lightning as Finn sped toward the main intersection.

"I think Jamie is in danger," Cole burst out. "I got a phone call from— Oh crap."

His abrupt exclamation came at the same time Finn slammed on the brakes. Cole hadn't bothered with his seatbelt, and he nearly smashed his head against the dash as the Jeep came to a screeching stop. A few yards from the intersection sat a white Honda Civic, its passenger door carelessly flung open.

Cole's heart thumped as he squinted for a better look. A dark head was slumped over the steering wheel. Valerie. He recognized the car, knew it had to be Teresa's sister in the driver's seat. The open passenger door indicated that someone else had been in the car with her.

Jamie.

After Finn drove the Jeep onto the shoulder of the road, Cole jumped out and ran to the white car, reaching it seconds before the sheriff lumbered up from behind. As Finn rounded the vehicle to examine any potential damage, Cole stuck a hand through the open window and touched Valerie Matthew's raven hair, nudging her gingerly. "Valerie. Valerie!"

She gave a strangled moan and then her head moved ever so slightly.

"Valerie, wake up. Where's Jamie?" Cole pleaded.

Another moan, followed by a whimper, and then she slowly looked up at him, her gray eyes glazed with confusion. "C-Cole?"

"Someone hit them from behind," Finn muttered, returning to the driver's side. "The bumper is all but gone."

Cole cursed at the news, then glanced back at the injured woman. "Valerie, are you okay?" He touched her hair again, lifted his hand and saw it was stained with blood.

"He...he knocked me out," Valerie murmured, awe and bewilderment ringing in her voice.

Cole choked down the lump of horror in his throat. "Who knocked you out, Val? Tell me what happened." When she just whimpered again, he grew frantic. "Valerie, where's Jamie?"

"He took her." A wobbly breath left her mouth. Shaking her head as if to clear it of cobwebs, she blinked several times, then focused her silvery gaze on Cole. "That guy who works for you...your assistant...he took Agent Crawford. He *took* her."

Chapter 16

"Get out of the car, Agent Crawford."

Jamie stared at the barrel of the gun, then up at the face of the man wielding it. For the hundredth time, she had trouble accepting that this was Ian Macintosh. Ian, the young man who'd been so pleasant to her the morning after the storm.

He looked like a completely different person. Brown eyes wild, boyish features twisted in a mask of evil loathing. She resisted the urge to rub her aching right temple, fearing any sudden movements would set him off. Or the gun. Her gun, she realized as she stared at the familiar Glock with the scratch on the butt. He must have grabbed it from her purse, after he'd run Valerie's car off the road.

She'd hit her head during the accident, and her memory was still fuzzy, but she recalled the crunching of metal, being propelled into the dashboard, then hearing muted footsteps and seeing Valerie droop forward. She remembered fumbling for her purse, and then…then Ian's face appeared in the passenger window, the door was thrown open and everything went black.

"I *said,* get out of the car!"

She blinked, trying to stay alert despite the throbbing of her head. She was in a beige sedan, most likely Ian's rental, and it was dark outside but not pitch black, which told her only a short amount of time had passed since he'd knocked her unconscious. The sun had just set when she'd gotten into Valerie's car, so it couldn't be later than seven o'clock, maybe eight.

"All right then, if that's how you want to be," Ian snapped.

The gun disappeared and he was out of the car, his footsteps thudding against the ground as he walked around to her side, opened the door and pulled her out of the sedan by her hair.

Her arm flew out in a desperate punch, but she'd instinctively used her right one, the injured one. Pain shot up to her shoulder and she sagged onto the gravel. She realized she'd landed on a driveway. Where the hell had he taken— She gasped when she caught sight of the commanding stone mansion.

She immediately figured out where they were. The house Cole had shared with Teresa.

"Why are you doing this?" she blurted out. "I thought you were loyal to Cole."

"Loyal to that murdering bastard?" Ian smirked. "You thought wrong, luv. Now get up."

She did as he asked, wishing she had a backup weapon right about now. She needed to neutralize this situation before Macintosh decided to pull the trigger.

He gestured her to move ahead of him. "Walk to the door."

Jamie used the walk along the limestone path to assess the situation. Ian definitely wasn't of sound mind, but his motive for doing this made no sense to her. Was he after Cole's company? Was he simply crazy?

His reasoning became clear as he made her open the double doors at the mansion's entrance, planted a hand on her back and shoved her into the house. Darkness shrouded them and then she heard a click and light flooded the impressive marble-lined parlor.

"You just couldn't do your damn job, could you, Agent?" Ian said with contempt in his voice. "Go through the doorway to the left."

He flicked another switch and Jamie found herself in an enormous living room with high ceilings and a gorgeous slate fireplace. Horror clogged her throat. This was the room in which Teresa Donovan had died. She glanced at the floor by the coffee table, growing sick when she saw the dark brown stain on the hardwood. Evidently the cleaning staff hadn't been able to scrub away the bloodstain.

Ian waved the gun. "Sit down."

When she moved to the couch, he barked at her again. "Not there. On the floor."

Nausea knotted around her insides as she realized where he wanted her to sit. Knowing she had to cooperate until she found a way out of this mess, she slowly moved across the room and sank down on the marred hardwood. Forced herself not to think about the pool of sticky blood that had once congealed there.

"You know," Ian said, his voice colder than a glacier, "I was quite pleased when you showed up in town. I thought, *Hey, now here's a smart woman, surely she'll see that he's a killer and send him to death row.*" He sneered at her. "But no, you had to go and screw the guy, didn't you, *Agent?*"

"Cole isn't a killer," she said quietly.

He went on as if she hadn't even spoken. "I tried to be nice to you! I left you that note, trying to help you get your priorities straight, but you ignored it! And then I tried warning you by messing with your car and you—"

"Warning?" she interrupted. "I could have died."

"And if you did, then the sheriff would have called in another agent, one capable of carrying out a simple task." Ian shrugged. "If you survived, I figured you'd skip town and let someone else take over, but you stuck around. I guess you do have a death wish."

"You shot me this morning." It was a statement, not a question.

"I missed," he confessed. "I wasn't planning on doing it—I was just keeping an eye on the house to make sure the bastard didn't try and skip town. Then you came outside and I decided, what the hell, might as well go for it. But you moved at the last second, and I'm afraid I'm not very good with guns." He wagged the weapon around as if to hammer the point home.

Jamie ran a hand through her hair, wincing when she unconsciously put her right arm to use again. She ignored the resulting pain and shot Ian a curious look. "So you're doing this because you hate Cole?"

His eyes flashed. "What I did before, I did because that son of a bitch needs to be in prison." His lips twisted in a malevolent smile. "But now…well, since you're obviously not going to punish him for his crime, *I'm* going to punish him."

She sighed. She didn't normally provoke psychopaths, but this was bordering on nonsensical. "I have no idea what you're saying, Ian. It's starting to sound a lot like crazy talk."

"Oh, I'm not making enough sense for you, Agent Crawford?" He made a tsking sound. "Not surprising, seeing as you're completely incompetent at your job. How about I spell it out for you then?"

"Please do," she couldn't help but bite out.

"Cole belongs in jail," Ian announced in a pleasant voice. "You're too stupid to put him there. Ergo, I've decided to dish out my own form of punishment." He leaned against the arm of the sofa, his gun hand swinging back and forth like a pendulum. "I'm going to make the bastard feel what it's like to lose the woman you love. Clear enough for you?"

Her mind reeled with shock. The woman you love? Who on earth—

"Oh, my God," she whispered. "You…you were one of the men Teresa had an affair with."

"Affair?" he roared. "We had more than an affair! We were in love! Those other men didn't matter, none of them mattered! *I* was the one she loved, and that son of a bitch took her away from me!"

She exhaled in frustration. "Cole didn't kill her."

"Yes, he *did!* He threatened to do it, too. She told me all about it. I was the one who told her to get the restraining order." Ian's cheeks turned red. "But it was too bloody late, wasn't it? He got to her! She tried to fight him off in the parking lot of the bar and he followed her home to finish the job."

"Cole was in the woods with Joe Gideon when Teresa died," Jamie said gently. "Gideon admitted to it."

"Then that bastard was paid off! Mr. Millionaire got to him," Ian snapped. "Now you know what? Shut up. I'm getting rather bored of this. Congratulations, luv, you did it, you got the bad guy to spend a few minutes outlining his motives and all that fun stuff. Now shut the hell up and lie down."

She faltered. "What?"

The gun in his hand jerked up. Even from her perch on the floor, she could see his fingers tightening over the trigger. "Lie. Down." He gestured to the bloodstain.

For the first time since he'd brought her here, Jamie experienced a rush of pure, unadulterated fear.

As she positioned herself the way Ian instructed, she realized with growing terror precisely what he was doing.

He was recreating Teresa's crime scene.

* * *

"I mean it, Donovan, either you tell me what's happening or I'll pull my gun out and shoot you in the knee."

It was an empty threat, but Cole heard the desperation in the sheriff's voice as the Jeep bounced over a pothole on the hasty ride to the house where Teresa died. Ian must have taken Jamie there. He would want to kill her in the place where Teresa had died. Cole felt it deep in his gut.

"My pilot called," Cole started.

"Your pilot? Is this let-me-brag-about-how-rich-I-am time or do you have a freaking point?"

He ignored the sarcasm. "My pilot, Pierre, called, wondering why I ordered the jet to stay in the hangar. Apparently Ian grounded the jet two days ago, when he told me he was flying back to Chicago. My pilots have been twiddling their thumbs at the hotel since then."

"You're talking about your assistant?" Finn sucked in a breath. "He lied about leaving town?"

Cole gave a sharp nod. "He was here, when Jamie had her accident, when she got shot, he was here the entire time." A sick feeling crept up his chest. "And it gets worse. After I spoke to Pierre, I called my P.I. to check into Ian's past flight records, to see if this has happened before."

"And it has."

"Yep. A dozen times over the past two years, he made visits to Serenade, when he was supposed to be somewhere else. Often he did stop off at the city I sent him to, then came here afterward."

Finn swore loudly. "And you didn't notice?"

"I was a little distracted, what with my cheating wife and tabloid-worthy divorce," he snapped, a sharp edge to his voice. "Besides, I trusted Ian. He's done a good job for me, especially in these past couple of years."

"Yeah, well, he was banging your wife."

"You made the connection too, huh?"

Cole battled an explosion of resentment at the thought. There was no other reason for Ian to be visiting Serenade without his boss. Unless he was involved with someone in town.

And seeing as Teresa slept with every man who so much as bumped into her, Ian must have been one of the men on her adultery list.

Swallowing down a lump of bitterness, Cole glanced at the sheriff. "That woman was poison. It wouldn't shock me in the least if she seduced my assistant. It would just be another fun way to get back at me."

"Did I ever apologize for not warning you ahead of time about Teresa?"

Cole's head swiveled in surprise. Was he hearing things?

"I'm serious," Finn continued, sounding gruff. "I always felt like an ass for not saying something before you married her."

It might not be an apology for treating him like a murderer, but Cole would take it. "I probably would have married her anyway," he said with a wry grin. "Your unsolicited advice would have just pushed me to the altar sooner."

"Well, nobody said you were smart."

Cole rolled his eyes, then went grave again as the Jeep reached the narrow slope leading up to the cliffside mansion. Lord, he hoped his instincts were right, that Ian had actually brought Jamie here. And he prayed that Ian hadn't hurt Jamie, that she was using her skills and good judgment to defuse whatever situation she'd found herself in. The irony of his thoughts didn't go unnoticed, either. An hour ago, he was accusing her of choosing her job over him. Now, he *prayed* that she relied on those professional instincts.

It might be the only way for her to stay alive.

"What the hell does Ian want with Jamie then?" Finn demanded.

"He's avenging Teresa's death." Cole's lungs burned as he inhaled. "He thinks I killed her."

"And now he's trying to punish you by killing Jamie?"

"Seems so. I think he's— No, pull over here," he said suddenly.

They had just reached the edge of the driveway, out of view from the house. Although Finn stopped the car and killed the engine, he glanced at Cole in suspicion. "What are you planning, Donovan?"

He exhaled the breath he'd been holding. "I need to go in there alone."

"What? No freaking way."

"If he sees you, he might panic and kill her." Cole forced himself not to dwell on *that* terrifying thought. "But if it's just me, I might be able to talk him down. Convince him I didn't murder Teresa."

"That's the dumbest plan I've ever heard," Finn said with a scowl. "You have no training, no experience with crazed criminals, no—"

"And you do? This is Serenade, for Chrissake. Crazed criminals don't live here."

"I still have the training," Finn insisted. He reached for the gun holstered at his hip. "I'm coming in with you."

"And then Jamie will get hurt. If he feels ambushed, he'll snap. Come on, Finn, think about it."

The sheriff went quiet for a moment, then let out a ragged breath as he saw Cole's point of view. "I'm not sitting out here in the car like a damned guard dog."

"I didn't expect you to. I just want to go in alone. You can come in on your own, get in position in case…in case you need to use that thing." He glanced at the weapon in Finn's hands. "But don't do anything until I get a handle on the situation. Promise me that."

"Fine." Finn reached for the door handle. "Let's do this."

Cole's entire body was riddled with dread as he got out of the Jeep. Finn hung back, letting Cole approach the house alone, in case Ian was watching from one of the windows. When Cole reached the top of the driveway, he spotted Ian's rental car. His instincts had been right then.

He winced as his shoes crunched over the gravel drive, then chided himself for it. Ian didn't have superhero hearing, for Chrissake.

Instead of walking up the path, he moved along the wall, creeping toward the front door as ice sludged through his veins. Christ, Finn was right. He wasn't a cop. How did he expect to do this on his own?

What if his inexperience got Jamie killed?

Willing away the fear gnawing at his gut, he reached the front door. His hand closed over the door handle. If he managed to gain the element of surprise here, maybe he could end it fast. Sneak up behind Ian, tackle him to the ground and knock him out with a chop to the back of the head. At least he felt confident in his karate chops, grateful for the martial arts classes he'd signed up for at his gym in Chicago.

The moment he slid through the front door, though, he realized he'd never had the element of surprise to begin with.

Ian had been expecting him.

"Come in already. I was waiting for you."

Cole nearly tripped as Ian's cheerful voice wafted in from the living room. He let out a sigh of defeat. So much for stealth mode. He suddenly wished the sheriff had given him a gun. Walking into the living room unarmed and at Ian's mercy was a disconcerting feeling. But for Jamie, he'd walk naked through fire. And for Jamie, he walked through that door.

"It's about time." Ian greeted him with a lopsided grin. "The show's about to begin."

Cole's assistant was sitting on the arm of one of the leather couches by the coffee table, his posture relaxed, as if he had all the time in the world. Cole's gaze absorbed the sight, then sought out Jamie. His heart stopped when he saw what Ian had done to her. She lay on the floor, her long auburn hair fanned out on the parquet. Cole nearly keeled over when he spotted the brown stain beneath her head. Blood. Oh Jesus. Ian had killed—

Dried blood, the remnant of Theresa's shooting. As he registered that fact, relief swept through him like a tornado, growing stronger when Jamie opened her eyes to give him an apologetic look, as if she were to blame for this lunacy.

He'd scold her about that later. Right now, he was just incredibly happy to see she was still alive.

"So, this is my punishment?" Cole's voice revealed none of the cold fear plaguing his body. "You're going to kill an innocent woman to avenge the death of a woman who didn't even love you?"

Ian's head shot up in shock. Evidently he hadn't expected Cole to go on the offensive like that, and rage slowly seeped into his features. "You don't know a goddamn thing about my relationship with Teri, you bastard!"

Teri?

"She *did* love me. You're the one whose guts she hated," Ian said, tossing Cole a nasty grin.

"She hated everyone," Cole answered quietly. "You know I'm right, Ian. Teresa was a bitter, angry woman who was incapable of love."

Ian let out a hearty laugh. "You didn't know her at all, Cole. The real Teresa, *my* Teresa, she was warm and loving and—"

"Sleeping with you to piss off her husband," Cole finished.

"She loved me! She used to call me the second you went out of town, begging me to come see her, to make love to her." Ian smirked. "She told me how bloody boring you were in bed, that no man made her feel the way I did."

Cole stared at his assistant with somber eyes, as an unexpected—and liberating—thought hit him. His entire marriage had been doomed from the start. He'd married a flawed, selfish and calculating woman who liked to toy with men, who was skilled at making others see what they wanted to see. His judgment hadn't failed him—she'd just been too damn good at pretending. Her manipulation of Ian proved that nobody stood a chance in the face of Teresa Matthews's noxious charm.

"She was the best thing that ever happened to me!" Ian's rant brought Cole back to the present. "And you took her away from me, all because you didn't want her to have your money. You threatened her, you attacked her in a parking lot and then put a bullet in her heart! So now—" the man practically cackled with joy "—now I'm going to take *her* away from *you*."

Cole shot a desperate glance at Jamie, who offered a vulnerable look in return. She didn't have a plan, he realized. How could she, with an injured shoulder and a head injury, which he deduced from the blood caked on her temple. Ian had the gun, the control, the madness.

Determination clamped down on Cole's chest. As Ian shifted the gun in Jamie's direction, Cole knew without a doubt that he wasn't going to let this happen. Screw everything else. Let Ian put a bullet in his brain. As long as Jamie managed to get away in the process, Cole was willing to sacrifice his life.

"You're right." He spoke in a loud, clear voice. "I did kill Teresa. I shot her in the heart, right where Jamie is lying."

With a strangled cry Ian spun around, his brown eyes glittering with horror. The gun in his hand wavered violently. "You bastard! I *knew* it."

"Yep," he said with a cavalier smile. "I killed that bitch."

A ferocious roar reverberated in the air as Ian staggered toward Cole like a man possessed. The gun continued to shake, Ian's eyes burning with a rage that could only be satisfied with the annihilation of the murderer in front of him.

"I killed her," Cole said again, a rush of serenity moving through him the closer Ian came.

Looking past Ian's shoulders, he saw Jamie rolling to the side, a blur of motion as she sprang to her feet, but he knew she wouldn't reach Ian in time. It was too late. Ian would win.

But so would Cole, because he would go to his grave with the knowledge that the woman he loved was all right.

As Ian raised his hand, Cole smiled at Jamie, hoping she could see in his eyes the emotions he couldn't voice, and then the gun in Ian's hand exploded and the bullet ripped through Cole's abdomen.

Chapter 17

Jamie hit the ground as the gunshot echoed in the room, followed by a second shot that made her ears ring. She lifted her head, shocked to see Ian falling to the floor with a thud. A second later Finn burst into the room, gun drawn, face hard with satisfaction.

She stumbled to her feet, only briefly glancing at Ian's lifeless body and the bullet hole right between his eyes. Finn had damn good aim, she had to give him that. But her focus wasn't on Ian or Finn or anything other than Cole. He'd stumbled to the floor from the force of Ian's shot and when she knelt down and looked at his ashen features, she could barely breathe. The blood drained from her face as fast it seemed to be draining from Cole's gut.

"Oh God, Finn! Help me stop this bleeding!"

Ripping off her jacket, she bunched it up in her hand and pressed it to Cole's stomach, applying as much pressure as she could. Cole's skin was clammy and pale, and he was unconscious. He was losing too much blood. It soaked right through the material of her jacket and stained her fingers.

"Ambulance," she choked out as Finn came to kneel beside her.

"Already on its way," he assured her, gently removing her hands so he could apply the pressure.

Her heart hammered in her chest and she battled a wave of dizziness as she slid behind Cole's head and lifted it into her lap. "Stay with me, Cole," she begged, stroking his cold face.

"He's lost a lot of blood," Finn muttered.

He was right, and there wasn't a damn thing they could do about it, not until the paramedics came and took over. As she caressed Cole's dark hair, she silently pleaded with him to fight. It wasn't lost on her that he was in this perilous position because of her. He'd antagonized Ian so the man wouldn't kill her. He'd taken a bullet for *her*.

Then another thought occurred to her. "Were you out there the entire time?" she demanded.

Finn nodded. "Donovan wanted to go in alone, so I hung back until I had no choice but to interfere. Macintosh was ready to take another shot when I fired my gun."

She wasn't worried about that—she knew killing Ian had been Finn's only option. "So you heard everything Cole said?" she asked slowly.

He gave another nod.

"Don't you dare arrest him," she said with a fierce look. "He didn't kill anyone, Finn. He just said that to—"

"I know," he interrupted, a soft look entering his eyes. "He said it to save you."

Satisfied that Finn wouldn't cause Cole any trouble, she turned her attention to the man she loved. The man whose blood was leaving yet another bloodstain on the floor of this beautiful room.

Don't die, Cole. Please don't die.

She realized with an aching heart that she couldn't lose him now. Not when she'd just found him. Found a man who excited her, who made her feel safe and happy. If having a future with him meant giving up her job, she'd do it in a heartbeat. All these years she'd worked herself to the bone, wanting to be successful, wanting to escape the miserable trailer park she'd grown up in, yet at this moment, she knew that none of it mattered. How could it, when she had nobody to share that success with?

The wail of sirens pierced through her thoughts. Relief swarmed her when the paramedics flew into the room a minute later, moving with skillful precision to load Cole onto a gurney and control the bleeding.

"Can I ride in the ambulance with him?" she asked one of the men.

They agreed to the request, and a few minutes later the ambulance sped toward the hospital in the next county. Apparently Dr. Bennett's clinic wasn't equipped to deal with injuries like Cole's, and Jamie went pale as she listened to the paramedic radio the hospital saying they needed an O.R. ready. Stat.

Surgery? She'd hoped that the bullet had gone through and through, but apparently that wasn't the case, and fear erupted in her belly, chilling her body.

When they reached the hospital she refused to let go of Cole's hand, until one of the nurses at the Emergency Room door forcibly disentangled their fingers and ushered Jamie to a sterile white waiting room. She was just collapsing onto one of the uncomfortable plastic chairs when Finn rushed into the room.

"They took him up to surgery," she said, looking up at him with dull eyes.

He was instantly by her side, taking both of her hands in

his. "He'll be okay, Jamie. If his gut's as thick as his skull, he'll be just fine, in fact."

She didn't smile at the joke. "What if he dies?" she whispered.

"He won't."

They didn't say much after that, just sat side by side in the room, as the clock hanging over the door ticked off the minutes. An hour passed, then two, and nobody came in with an update. Finn was still holding her hand, warming it between his fingers as ice continued to slither through her veins.

"He risked his life for me," she said, tears welling up in her eyes.

Finn squeezed her fingers. "He'll be okay," he reiterated.

It took two more hours before someone finally came. A doctor wearing a white coat greeted them with a tired smile, and Jamie jumped to her feet. "Is he all right?" she demanded.

"He's going to be just fine."

She sagged against Finn in relief.

"There was some internal bleeding caused by the bullet, and we had to give him three transfusions for the loss of blood, but he pulled through." The doctor looked proud as he added, "Mr. Donovan is a fighter. A lot of patients display a will to live, but in this case, it was more than that." He shook his head. "It was as if he simply refused to give up, as if there was no other choice."

"Can I see him?" Jamie asked through her tears.

"He's in recovery right now, and normally we only allow family members to—"

"I'm his fiancée," she lied, ignoring Finn's surprised gasp.

"Oh. Then I'm sure we'll be able to accommodate you, Ms....?"

"Crawford. Jamie Crawford."

"Come this way, Ms. Crawford."

She followed the doctor down the fluorescent-lit corridor toward the elevator bank. As they rode up to the third floor, she wiped her tears away with the sleeve of her blouse and uttered a silent prayer, this one thanking God for saving Cole's life. Upstairs the doctor led her to a private room at the end of the hall and held open the door.

"He'll be unconscious for a while," he warned.

"I don't mind. I want to be there when he wakes up." She smiled, fighting a new batch of tears. "Thank you for saving his life, Doctor."

"It's my job." His mouth tilted in a smile. "But it's my pleasure."

Unashamed of the tears sliding down her cheeks, she shook the doctor's hand and walked into Cole's room.

It felt like someone was hammering jagged nails into his stomach. That was the only thought Cole had as he navigated through a maze of unconsciousness and opened his eyes. Once the light assaulted his vision, he flinched and slammed his eyelids closed, growing nauseous as his head began to spin.

A husky laugh tickled his ear. "Seriously? You're just going to open your eyes like that and then go back to sleep? You're such a tease."

His mouth lifted in a smile and this time he fought through the pain to pry his eyes open. And then there she was, her lavender eyes swimming with love and concern, that gorgeous auburn hair cascading over her shoulders like a silky curtain.

"Hey," he said, wincing at the gravelly rasp to his voice.

"Hey yourself." He felt her hand on his, and although her skin was cold, it brought a rush of warmth to his throbbing abdomen. "You had me worried there for a while. How dare you lose so much blood?"

"I'm sorry," he murmured. "I'll try to lose an acceptable amount next time."

"Next time? I don't think so, Donovan. You're never getting shot again, as long as I have anything to say about it."

A comfortable silence fell between them, as the teasing faded away and a serious air crept in.

"Ian?" Cole asked, closing his eyes in anticipation.

"He's gone. Finn shot him."

Despite all the turmoil Ian had caused, Cole still experienced a flicker of regret at the loss of his assistant. Ian had been invaluable to him for so many years, at least before Teresa had lured him to the dark side and corrupted his mind.

"I need to notify his mother."

Jamie replied in a firm voice. "That can wait. Right now, you need to worry about getting better. You almost died."

"You almost died too."

"But you came to my rescue," she said, her eyes glistening as she squeezed his hand again. "That was a dumb thing to do, by the way. Killers 101—never antagonize the person holding a gun."

He laughed, and was rewarded by a jolt of pain. "I guess I missed the class."

"Don't worry, I'll teach you everything I know." She cast him a faint smile. "In case you didn't read between the lines, that means I'm not going anywhere."

Something shifted in his chest. "No?"

"No," she said softly. "I love you, Cole, and I don't care how many issues you still have over your ex-wife. I'll help you work through them."

"There's nothing to work through."

She stared at him in puzzlement.

"During the confrontation with Ian...I realized something." He struggled to sit up, ignoring the agony that sliced into his stomach. "Teresa was a spectacular liar and she fooled me, just like she fooled Ian. I can either kick myself for it for the rest of my life, or I can let the anger and insecurity go. Right now."

"Do you really think you can do that?"

"I don't think I have a choice." The corner of his mouth lifted wryly. "If I want to start a life with the woman I love, I can't be harping on the past. I have to focus on the future."

Jamie's breath hitched.

"You heard me," he said with a hoarse laugh. "I love you, Jamie."

He gripped her hand and brought it up to his heart so she could feel its rapid beating. "And I don't want you to quit your job," he added. When she blinked in surprise, he gave her a pointed look. "Don't tell me you weren't considering it. I can read your mind, sweetheart."

"I just don't want anything to come between us," she confessed. "I want a husband and babies and a gloriously happy future—with you, Cole. But I don't want you to think my career or anything else comes first for me. If we're together, you'll always come first."

"I know that now. But I also know your work is a part of you, and I would never ask you to stop doing it." He suddenly grinned. "But how would you feel if I stopped doing mine?"

Her eyes widened. "What?"

"I keep thinking about that offer from Lewis Limited," he admitted. "Not sure it's even legit, seeing as Ian was the one who told me about it, but if they're truly interested in buying Donovan Enterprises...I think I might sell. I never thought I'd ever say this, but I'm exhausted. I've worked myself ragged trying to build an empire, but these past weeks, I've been in Serenade, and the downtime has been nice...more than nice, actually."

"So you're just going to sell out? Give it all up?"

"I only got into the business to spite my father. And the

more I think about it, the more I realize I don't want to be like him. A workaholic, a businessman first." He sat up higher, the pain in his body fading as an awe-inspiring thought hit him. "I think it might be fun to be a stay-at-home dad."

Jamie's jaw dropped. He was actually quite surprised it didn't meet the floor. "Are you kidding me?"

"Nope." He grinned again. "My dad was never around for me when I was a kid. I don't want to be an absentee father, and since you want to have a ton of babies…"

More tears spilled from her eyes. "God, Cole, I didn't think it was possible to love you any more than I already do, but now…"

"Now you pictured me as a sexy dad and couldn't control yourself?"

She laughed through her tears. "Something like that."

"Good." He moved a little bit closer to her. "Now come here and let me kiss you. I'm feeling kind of sleepy and don't want to pass out until we seal this engagement with a kiss."

"Engagement?" She raised an eyebrow. "Did I miss the proposal?"

"Oh, that." He paused for effect. "Will you marry me?"

"I'll need a few days to think about it," she said primly.

"You're not serious, right?"

"Of course I'm not serious." She slid toward him, lowering her head until their faces were inches apart. "And of course I'll marry you."

Then she bridged the distance between their lips and sealed it with a kiss.

Epilogue

Finn left the hospital torn between breaking out in a grin or a grimace. He was a tad pissed at himself for being so damn happy that Donovan had survived, but he couldn't stop the annoying burst of joy. Maybe he and Donovan would never be the best of friends, but the man had taken a bullet to save Finn's closest friend and that was something Finn would always be grateful for.

As he stepped out into the cool night air, he tucked his hands into the pockets of his jacket and stared up at the inky sky. Christ, what a night. Firing his weapon wasn't something he did often, and his hands still shook with regret as he thought about the life he'd taken tonight. Ian Macintosh hadn't deserved to die. He should've been punished for his attempts on Jamie's life, but for falling into Teresa Donovan's web? That was something Finn wouldn't wish on anyone.

The killer's still out there.

The obtrusive thought slipped to the forefront of his brain, bringing a sigh to his lips. Jamie had told him that Ian had confessed to leaving her the note, messing with her car and taking a shot at her, though how Ian had procured a gun to shoot her with was still a mystery. But Cole's assistant hadn't murdered Teresa. Ian had been so overcome with grief that he'd needed to blame someone—and so he'd blamed Cole, believing the meager evidence against his boss meant Donovan was the killer.

Finn had believed it too, but he wasn't so sure anymore. Now that Gideon had grudgingly backed up Cole's alibi, and after seeing Donovan risk his life for Jamie, Finn's conviction in the man's guilt had wavered. No, not wavered. Disappeared.

Damn it, he didn't think Cole was a killer.

Which meant the real culprit was still on the loose.

But how the hell could he catch this guy? This case was nothing but a damn headache. A murder weapon that had mysteriously made an appearance. A mayor breathing down his neck to close this case.

If only he had what he actually wanted—a lead.

As if a higher power had picked up on his distress, the cell phone in his pocket started to vibrate, making his hand tingle.

He glanced at the caller ID, then lifted the phone to his ear. "Hey, Anna, what's up?"

"Is Mr. Donovan okay?" was the first thing she asked.

"He'll be fine," Finn assured her. "The surgery went well, and he's in recovery as we speak."

"That's good news." Anna's voice grew serious. "That's not actually why I called, though."

Finn was instantly on guard. "What's going on?"

"Um, well…"

"Quit stalling, Deputy Holt. Tell me."

"The forensic reports came in."

He blinked. "At midnight?"

"Well, no, the lab tech faxed them this afternoon, but I

only checked the fax machine now. With all the commotion, you know, the murder weapon at the dump, Cole's interrogation, the false emergency call…I kind of forgot."

"It's all right, Anna, you don't have to explain. Just tell me what the reports say."

"Um…"

"Anna."

A heavy breath sounded in his ear. "Okay, well, the DNA under Teresa's fingernails was inconclusive. There wasn't enough of it to get a clean sample."

Finn hid his surprise. *There goes that.* Cole and his attorney would be pleased to know that there was no DNA evidence linking Cole to the crime. In Finn's book, that meant Donovan was officially cleared. With an alibi and lack of forensic evidence, there was nothing to indicate Cole's guilt.

"What else?" he asked his deputy.

"Most of the fingerprints and hair samples belonged to Teresa, except…" She halted abruptly.

Apprehension curled around his spine. "Except what?"

"There was a match on the partial print on the coffee table, and one of the hair samples near the body."

"Spit it out, Anna."

"Sheriff…the print and DNA belonged to Sarah Connelly." Another shaky breath. "I'm so sorry. I know that Ms. Connelly is—"

But Finn had already hung up the phone, and then he just stared at it for several heart-wrenching seconds.

Sarah?

His Sarah?

Oh Lord.

And just when he thought things couldn't possibly get worse.

* * * * *

SUSPENSE

Heartstopping stories of intrigue and mystery—
where true love always triumphs.

COMING NEXT MONTH
AVAILABLE DECEMBER 27, 2011

#1687 TOOL BELT DEFENDER
Lawmen of Black Rock
Carla Cassidy

#1688 SPECIAL AGENT'S PERFECT COVER
Perfect, Wyoming
Marie Ferrarella

#1689 SOLDIER'S RESCUE MISSION
H.O.T. Watch
Cindy Dees

#1690 THE HEARTBREAK SHERIFF
Small-Town Scandals
Elle Kennedy

REQUEST YOUR FREE BOOKS!
2 FREE NOVELS PLUS 2 FREE GIFTS!

ROMANTIC
SUSPENSE
Sparked by Danger, Fueled by Passion.

YES! Please send me 2 FREE Harlequin® Romantic Suspense novels and my 2 FREE gifts (gifts are worth about $10). After receiving them, if I don't wish to receive any more books, I can return the shipping statement marked "cancel." If I don't cancel, I will receive 4 brand-new novels every month and be billed just $4.49 per book in the U.S. or $5.24 per book in Canada. That's a saving of at least 14% off the cover price! It's quite a bargain! Shipping and handling is just 50¢ per book in the U.S. and 75¢ per book in Canada.* I understand that accepting the 2 free books and gifts places me under no obligation to buy anything. I can always return a shipment and cancel at any time. Even if I never buy another book, the two free books and gifts are mine to keep forever.

240/340 HDN FEFR

Name _____ (PLEASE PRINT)

Address _____ Apt. #

City _____ State/Prov. _____ Zip/Postal Code

Signature (if under 18, a parent or guardian must sign)

Mail to the **Reader Service:**

IN U.S.A.: P.O. Box 1867, Buffalo, NY 14240-1867
IN CANADA: P.O. Box 609, Fort Erie, Ontario L2A 5X3

Not valid for current subscribers to Harlequin Romantic Suspense books.

Want to try two free books from another line?
Call 1-800-873-8635 or visit www.ReaderService.com.

* Terms and prices subject to change without notice. Prices do not include applicable taxes. Sales tax applicable in N.Y. Canadian residents will be charged applicable taxes. Offer not valid in Quebec. This offer is limited to one order per household. All orders subject to credit approval. Credit or debit balances in a customer's account(s) may be offset by any other outstanding balance owed by or to the customer. Please allow 4 to 6 weeks for delivery. Offer available while quantities last.

Your Privacy—The Reader Service is committed to protecting your privacy. Our Privacy Policy is available online at www.ReaderService.com or upon request from the Reader Service.

We make a portion of our mailing list available to reputable third parties that offer products we believe may interest you. If you prefer that we not exchange your name with third parties, or if you wish to clarify or modify your communication preferences, please visit us at www.ReaderService.com/consumerchoice or write to us at Reader Service Preference Service, P.O. Box 9062, Buffalo, NY 14269. Include your complete name and address.

HRS11B

INTRIGUE

Brittany Grayson survived a horrible ordeal at the hands
of a serial killer known as The Professional…
who's after her now?

Harlequin® Romantic Suspense presents a new installment
in Carla Cassidy's reader-favorite miniseries,
LAWMEN OF BLACK ROCK.

Enjoy a sneak peek of
TOOL BELT DEFENDER.

Available January 2012
from Harlequin® Romantic Suspense.

"**B**rittany?" His voice was deep and pleasant and made her realize she'd been staring at him openmouthed through the screen door.

"Yes, I'm Brittany and you must be…" Her mind suddenly went blank.

"Alex. Alex Crawford, Chad's friend. You called him about a deck?"

As she unlocked the screen, she realized she wasn't quite ready yet to allow a stranger inside, especially a male stranger.

"Yes, I did. It's nice to meet you, Alex. Let's walk around back and I'll show you what I have in mind," she said. She frowned as she realized there was no car in her driveway. "Did you walk here?" she asked.

His eyes were a warm blue that stood out against his tanned face and was complemented by his slightly shaggy dark hair. "I live three doors up." He pointed up the street to the Walker home that had been on the market for a while.

"How long have you lived there?"

"I moved in about six weeks ago," he replied as they

walked around the side of the house.

That explained why she didn't know the Walkers had moved out and Mr. Hard Body had moved in. Six weeks ago she'd still been living at her brother Benjamin's house trying to heal from the trauma she'd lived through.

As they reached the backyard she motioned toward the broken brick patio just outside the back door. "What I'd like is a wooden deck big enough to hold a barbecue pit and an umbrella table and, of course, lots of people."

He nodded and pulled a tape measure from his tool belt. "An outdoor entertainment area," he said.

"Exactly," she replied and watched as he began to walk the site. The last thing Brittany had wanted to think about over the past eight months of her life was men. But looking at Alex Crawford definitely gave her a slight flutter of pure feminine pleasure.

Will Brittany be able to heal in the arms of Alex, her hotter-than-sin handyman...or will a second psychopath silence her forever? Find out in
TOOL BELT DEFENDER
Available January 2012
from Harlequin® Romantic Suspense
wherever books are sold.

Harlequin

SPECIAL EDITION

Life, Love and Family

Karen Templeton

introduces

The FORTUNES *of* TEXAS: Whirlwind Romance

When a tornado destroys Red Rock, Texas, Christina Hastings finds herself trapped in the rubble with telecommunications heir Scott Fortune. He's handsome, smart and everything Christina has learned to guard herself against. As they await rescue, an unlikely attraction forms between the two and Scott soon finds himself wanting to know about this mysterious beauty. But can he catch Christina before she runs away from her true feelings?

FORTUNE'S CINDERELLA

Available December 27th wherever books are sold!

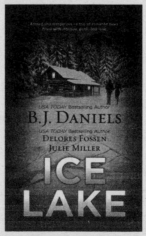